Penguin Books

SEDUCED by FAME

Isla Fisher was born in 1976, in the old walled city of Muscat in the Sultanate of Oman. She was the last non-Arab to be born there. She travelled for some years in Asia before settling with her Scottish family in Western Australia. She was educated at Methodist Ladies College in Perth and spent many of her schooldays, from thirteen years upwards, on various film sets. She left home halfway through year twelve to take up a part in 'Paradise Beach', filmed on the Gold Coast of Queensland. Six months later she joined the cast of 'Home and Away', where she is still a regular.

Isla lives in Sydney and frequently returns to Perth to visit her parents and four brothers. Her hobbies are horse riding, writing and reading.

SEDUCED by FAME

isla fisher

Penguin Books

PUFFIN BOOKS

Published by the Penguin Group
Penguin Books Ltd, 27 Wrights Lane, London W8 5TZ, England
Penguin Books USA Inc., 375 Hudson Street, New York, New York 10014, USA
Penguin Books Australia Ltd, Ringwood, Victoria, Australia
Penguin Books Canada Ltd, 10 Alcorn Avenue, Toronto, Ontario, Canada M4V 3B2
Penguin Books (NZ) Ltd, 182–190 Wairau Road, Auckland 10, New Zealand

Penguin Books Ltd, Registered Offices: Harmondsworth, Middlesex, England

First published in Australia by Penguin Books, 1995
Published in the UK by Puffin Books, 1996
5 7 9 10 8 6

Typeset in 11.5/14 pt Times Roman by Midland Typesetters
Printed in England by Clays Ltd, St Ives plc

To my mother,
who's never worn squeaky rubber gloves in her life
and who'd rather read a good book
than clean the house.
So inspiring!

1

She woke up, heart thumping, damp with sweat. Keeping her eyes tightly shut, she slammed off the alarm clock. Gradually her heartbeats slowed. It was that dream again. The one where she's trapped with her boyfriend Wayne in his Commodore. Outside she can see her family and his, faces pressed to the windows mouthing 'congratulations'. She's wearing a cheap lace wedding dress, so tight she can hardly breathe. So she screams, but there's no sound and everyone is grinning and throwing confetti . . .

Jade Silver opened her eyes, letting the familiar objects swim into focus. The morning sun lit up a poster of her heart-throb, Daniel Hunter. She smiled right back at him. He was so dark, so handsome and so sun-tanned that he might have been a Pirate

King on the high seas. *Oh kidnap me*, she thought, *rescue me. Leap aboard the Commodore and drag me off to a desert island!* The alarm clock screeched again, a reminder call.

Downstairs she heard her sister Samantha whingeing about school. Her petulant little voice drifted up the stairs.

'Jade left school early, why can't I?'

'Because if you don't go to school you'll never get a job, sweetheart,' her mother replied patiently. She was always patient with Samantha and the twins.

'Jade got a job,' the shrill voice persisted.

'Not a *real* one.'

Jade wrenched at the blankets and dragged herself out of bed. No real job! Why couldn't anyone see she didn't need a job? She had a dream, a dream she'd nurtured since she was a child. Jobs were for people who gave up on their dreams!

She gazed unhappily into the mirror. White-blonde hair fell heavily down her shoulders and over one eye. Pushing it back, she examined her face critically. Would you hire this girl to star in your next movie? *Probably not*, she thought miserably. Her hair was so white they called her Albino at school. Her eyelashes and eyebrows were invisible and her eyes were the palest translucent green, like glass pebbles washed up on the shore. As for her skin! It was arctic white all year round, except when she blushed or sat out too long in the sun. Then she turned magenta.

2

Her agent said she wasn't Australian enough. 'Not much call for Nordic Goddesses, darling. Why not stick to your books? You could always go on to drama college, then you'd have a decent qualification behind you.'

What difference did it make what she looked like? She was an actor, not a model. So it was even more hurtful when he added ...

'... if you lost a bit of weight, you'd get modelling work. You're tall enough.'

She stared determinedly at her reflection. *I shall make it, whatever they say, however long it takes.* As famous as Nicole Kidman without having to marry Tom Cruise. She stuck out her tongue, then dived into the bathroom.

Switching on the shower, she let the scalding water sting her back. A squirt of pearly shampoo massaged into her hair filled the shower with rose-perfumed steam. She loved the luxurious scent of roses, loved feeling pampered and expensive. Not much chance of that happening in this house! It was usually littered with washing and Lego, and the closest she ever came to pampering was a packet of Tim Tams to herself. She sighed, held her face up to the warm cascade and thought about her private fantasy, the Plan. It always soothed her to go over the Plan, especially now when it was going so well.

She remembered when it all started, soon after Samantha was born. Her mother stayed in hospital for two weeks, and Jade slept in front of the TV.

When they finally came home, baby Samantha was sickly and no one had any time for Jade. Mum didn't even notice her hunched up in the beanbag in front of the box. Later, when the twins were born, it was 'Fetch this, carry that, you've got to help Mum'. The only escape was watching TV. Hiding in her duvet, she wept through old movies and daytime soaps. She yearned to be in 'The Brady Bunch' with a real TV Mom and Dad. Or the Cosby family. Everyone looked beautiful and happy on TV. While her mum and step-father yelled, TV people danced and laughed and loved each other. If only she could join them!

Once she asked her step-father if she could visit the Cosbys. He said, 'They're just actors; it's not real.' But she knew it was real, more real than crying babies and dirty nappies. So to get there she'd have to be an actor? Well, that shouldn't be so hard. 'What do actors do?' she asked her mother. 'Pretend to be other people,' came the answer. And she did. Whenever she could escape from house-work, she hibernated in her bedroom trying on facial expressions, voices, accents, walks. Some-times she wasn't sure who she was any more; there was always some other character to slip on that fitted the situation better. Eventually her friends gave up and her Mum despaired. But it didn't matter. She was going to be an actress. She knew it as she knew her name was Jade Silver.

She was nearly fourteen when the Plan started to take shape. Players, Melbourne's top theatrical agency, accepted her on condition she took drama lessons at their private theatre. The lessons weren't cheap and the train ride to Melbourne took almost forty minutes. So she got a job washing cars for Wayne's father, down at Gorilla Motors. From that moment the die was cast.

By the time she was fifteen even Mum, who had an endless capacity for self-deception, gave up talking about University. Jade left school, served in a restaurant and carried on with acting classes. Her idol, Jodie Foster, said success came when you were ready for it. Soon, she thought, please let it be soon.

'Switch the bloody shower off!' Her step-father thought one shower a week was enough for Jade. 'My water bills look like the national debt. And hurry up, I'm leaving in one minute.'

Jade twisted the shower lever and groped for a towel. It was like being in a sauna. Drying off a patch of steam in the mirror, she saw her face was as red as a tomato.

'Jay-jay,' Samantha whined from behind the bathroom door. 'Can I open that letter on the hall table, the one addressed to you?'

'Leave it alone,' she screeched, grabbing a towel and flinging the bathroom door open. A blast of cold air made her teeth chatter. 'Touch that letter and you're dead.' Her eyes bored into Samantha.

'Tomato face,' Samantha grinned and darted back into the bedroom they shared.

It was a letter from her agent. It had arrived

yesterday, but she was too scared to open it. As long as it stayed closed, she could dream a little longer. It was hopeless, really. A major TV drama was holding a nationwide search for the next female lead. Her agent had advised against it.

'TV celebrities are famous for having nice teeth. Do you want that?'

Well, actually she did. She would have killed for the part. Not because of the show; television no longer enchanted her. It was film or stage work she wanted. But the show's lead was Daniel Hunter. She'd adored him since he first appeared on the screen almost three years ago.

'Perhaps I could audition for the experience,' she suggested.

'You and a zillion others.'

She could hear him lighting a cigarette. 'Please send my details in, please, please, please . . .'

'Jade, these shows lock you into long contracts. You get over-exposed and typecast. And in any case, you don't have the right look.'

'What's wrong with my look?' Jade felt that awful sinking feeling whenever her appearance was mentioned.

'Nothing. A bit tall maybe, not the cute dolly look these shows want. And your colouring is, well, different. Anyway, you'll be up against every would-be starlet under twenty in Australia.'

Jade didn't trust herself to speak. Her own agent had no faith in her!

But he relented. 'Oh, all right. Just don't hold your breath.'

Then, wonder of wonders: she'd been called – a cattle call with hundreds of others that gave her two minutes alone with Maggie Gold, the casting agent. Most of the others were in for ten, so of course Maggie mustn't have liked her. But she could still dream . . .

'Where the hell are you, Jade?' Her step-father's voice was up a few decibels. Patience was not one of his strong points.

'I'm ready. Just helping Sam with her plaits,' she lied, rushing into their room to dress.

Seconds later, she leapt down the stairs two at a time, flicked up the letter, stuffed it into her bag and joined her step-father in his old Volvo. Trapped, she was forced to listen to one of his favourite lectures on Responsibility, followed by Gratitude. He was like that. He only spoke in capital letters. As if whatever he said was More Important Than Anything.

By the time she reached Giorgio's Restaurant, he'd made her feel like a Total Reject. *Oh well*, she thought, *might as well prove him right*. With trembling fingers, she took out the letter.

'Are you here to work or read your love letters?' Giorgio glowered at her.

She thrust it nervously back into her bag.

'And stay on this afternoon, I need you in the kitchen.'

'There's no need to shout. I've had my

step-dad yelling at me all morning.'

'If you were my daughter I'd have you married off by now. My wife was eighteen when we married. And in her prime.' He reached over to pat her bottom.

'That's sexual harassment!'

'A few kids to look after would sort you out.' He turned back to his garlic, chopping with ferocious swiping movements.

Jade tied on a clean white apron and pinned the lacy top half to her chest. 'And I can't stay late. Got a modelling job.'

'You can model for me any time,' he leered.

'Speak to my agent.' She stalked off. Giorgio had a problem with his hormones.

At four o'clock, she hung up her apron and headed towards the Borringup Hypermart for the ghastly Miss Dairy Queen promotion. Since she'd left school two years ago she'd done a few retail promotions. They paid well, but they could be so humiliating.

The supermarket was filled with housewives trundling huge trolleys of food. Suppressing a shudder, she dived into the changing room, stripped naked and pulled on a cream, chiffon-draped swimming costume. Then, flicking back her hair, she gazed in despair at her reflection. *I'm so pale, I look like a bottle of milk*, she moaned, *and there will be no use crying when I get spilled if that letter is a rejection!* She glanced uneasily at the envelope sticking out of her bag. *Time to get real, Jade!*

'Are you ready, Miss Dairy Queen?'

There was sarcasm in the photographer's voice. *Don't patronise me*, she muttered to herself, rummaging in her make-up bag for the lustre-lash mascara. Carefully she outlined her eyes with an emerald kohl stick she'd pinched from her mother. Players had taught her how to make her eyes and mouth more prominent. Stepping back, she hardly recognised herself. High cheek bones, up-swept eyes like a Siamese cat and a full-lipped, curving mouth. She scowled in disgust, hating the look. Even wearing lipstick felt disgusting, as if she'd eaten too many chips.

She fluffed up her hair and licked her lips, then stepped out into the office.

'Wow, er Miss er ... Dairy Queen!' The manager, a gangly young man with a pony-tail, gazed at her, eyes on stalks. He didn't recognise her.

'It's me, Jade. We went to school together. You used to bully me on the bus when I was in year eight.'

'Albino!' The shock of recognition made him sit down.

'Over here, in front of the goat's cheese,' the photographer's spiteful voice rang out. Jealous!

It took almost two hours to complete the shot. Two hours of smiling, holding out cartons of milk and fetta cheese towards the camera. *Years of acting and voice classes for this*, she thought. Her feet were killing her and there was a growing sense of dread about the unopened letter in her bag. *Now,*

9

do it now, she urged herself. *No, later*, another voice inside answered.

'Okay, it's a wrap!'

What about a 'thank you, Jade', she thought, kicking off her shoes and heading back to the changing room. *I'm just a lump of meat, or a carton of cream, to him. To all of them*, she thought. *One day I'll be a famous actor, then I'll never have to stand around grinning in a stupid costume ever again*. The rain was drumming hard on the metal roof and blurring the view of the High Street as she dashed in to the manager's office.

He was waiting to pounce on her from behind the filing cabinet.

'You look tired!' he smarmed. 'Can I get you anything? A drink, or something to eat?'

Jade looked directly into his eyes. Was that real concern, or just the usual suck-up? For some time now she'd noticed men hanging on her every word and staring. She decided he was a sleaze and shook her head briefly.

'I'd like to make it up for the bullying on the bus,' he continued, undeterred.

'Forget it,' Jade answered. 'I have,' and she disappeared into the changing room. As she pulled on her old jeans, she found herself shaking with apprehension. The letter's sharp, ice-white edge poked out of the bag. She could see her agent's logo on the corner: two actor's masks, one grinning like a maniac, the other suicidal. *Which one will be me?* she wondered.

'Can I give you a lift?' The manager's muffled voice came through the door.

'Sorry, I have a jealous boyfriend,' she answered automatically, picking up the letter as if it were a live bomb. This was ridiculous. She was starting to believe the unbelievable. According to the Plan, success wasn't scheduled until after a few small but brilliantly played parts in which she came to the attention of an international director, at roughly twenty-two. Almost four years away.

'If you still live at Borringup End, it's on my way,' he persisted.

She pushed it back. Not the place to end this fantasy. Better read it on the train. She ducked out of the room, leaving the manager mouthing his last offer, and dashed into the street.

For several minutes she stood on the pavement, waiting for a break in the stream of traffic. Occasionally she stepped back to avoid waves of muddy water thrown up by truck wheels. Rain dripped down the back of her neck and whipped across her cheeks. The traffic lights changed, and Jade seized her chance. She was breathless by the time she leapt on to the train as it slowly eased out of the station. Pushing her way through the crowded compartments, she spotted a solitary window seat waiting for her, as if she'd called ahead. 'Thank you, God,' she murmured triumphantly, climbing over suitcases and outstretched legs to claim it.

Flopping down, she raked her fingernails through her scalp and released the full weight of silvery hair from her collar. Then, rummaging in her bag for a clean tissue, she dried her hands and face. Settled at last, she pushed her hand deep into her bag and reached for it. For a moment, she fought to contain a mixture of emotions. Fear, hysteria, hope? Finally, taking a deep breath, she pulled it out, and with trembling fingers tore open the envelope. Hardly daring to breathe, she began to read.

'Dear Jade, Incredible news. Maggie Gold & Associates tell me they liked you. They are short-listing you and three other girls in this State, as well as girls in other States. So you're in with a chance, a small chance anyway ...'

Suddenly, she was in danger of bursting with excitement. She rested her head against the seat, closed her eyes and let an explosion of joy flood her body. She could see the producer of 'Sunshine Coast' shaking her hand, the deal done. She began to hyperventilate. *Jade, not yet, wait until the contract's signed.* She wrenched herself back to the letter.

'... on Saturday 18 September. You will be auditioning with Daniel Hunter, whose character Jason ...'

As if she didn't know who Daniel Hunter was!

'.... . will have a relationship with Kerry, the character you are reading for.'

If I get no further than the audition, I'll die happy. Jade squirmed in her seat with excitement, with pleasure, with sheer terror.

'Please learn the following scripts. They'll see you at three-thirty in the Old Melbourne Theatre in Thomas Lane. Yours sincerely . . . '

Her eyes followed diamonds of rain skating nervously down the window. The sun was glittering through the clouds, creating myriads of tiny rainbows blotting out the dull red suburbs. She thought of fame and fortune. Suddenly she wanted them with a hunger she could taste. For as long as she could remember she'd been mesmerised by the glamorous red-lipped beauties who filled her TV screen and pouted at her from magazines. Could she ever be one of them?

But they like me. Raising her eyes triumphantly, she met the dull stare of an exhausted-looking housewife, surrounded by packages on the seat opposite. She smiled brilliantly. *They like me.*

Closing her eyes, she pictured herself in a glimmering evening dress, gliding out of a Cadillac and swaying gracefully through waiting photographers and journalists. She must keep practising the model's walk. When she tried it on Wayne, he accused her of being drunk.

She saw herself entering a cinema foyer, with giant-sized posters blazing out her face and name. Tonight is the Gala Opening Night! Crowds gather, the glitterati of New York. Her escort for the evening waits at the foot of the stairs, immaculate in a white tuxedo. His handsome face turns slowly to greet her . . . .

'The next stop is Borringup End.' The

electronic voice jolted her back. Leaping to her feet, she tripped over one of the packages, half falling onto the tired housewife.

'You were dreaming,' the woman spoke kindly.

'Not for much longer,' Jade laughed, and she dashed out of the train. A vast magical rainbow stretched across the pale grey sky, like a Walt Disney cartoon. *A sign!* she exulted. *The pot of gold is waiting for me!* Her footsteps quickened, beating a rhythm with her boots on the station steps. She flipped back her hair, a smile curving her lips. A gang of schoolboys trudging past barracked and whistled. She lifted her chin, green eyes sparkling against her creamy complexion. Schoolboys were definitely not part of the Plan. In fact men didn't figure at all.

The Plan only included fantasies like Daniel Hunter, safely contained in a poster. A sudden thought jolted. How would she ever be able to hide the crush she'd had on him since she was fifteen? Her heart speeded up just thinking about him. Even her face grew hot. Stopping, she threw her hands up to the heavens. Please God, let them cast me, she implored, I swear I'll be completely professional. He'll never know how I feel. I'll work so hard, I'd even give *him* up to be a success!

The rainbow arched magnificently above her, pure bands of coloured light. Then a distant crack of thunder, a faint flickering of lightning, and the first splodges of rain fell. She dashed through the

14

turnstile and joined the rest of the commuters spilling out into Railway Terrace. *I'll never let myself end up like them*, she thought, remembering the tired-looking woman on the train. Or Mum. Dragged down by marriage and babies, no time or money to enjoy life.

She darted into an alley, a short cut to her house. Rain poured heavily from the gutters and soaked the fast-food cartons littering the alley. But she was too busy straining to see her rainbow, fading now against the darkening sky. Then, taking a flying leap off the pavement, she danced into her street.

And there was Wayne, lovingly soaping his precious car in the middle of the downpour. Poor old Wayne!

'Hi, mate,' he called out. 'Did you get the part?'

'Maybe.' She kept going. Any encouragement and he'd be over for a beer. People thought they were together. In a way they were, but like brother and sister. Their families had been friends since childhood and they sort of drifted around occasionally. Jade found him useful for keeping other men away and picking her up from the theatre at night. And Wayne seemed perfectly happy with Jade as a decoration for his Commodore. There was a huge, framed photo of her swinging her legs elegantly out of the car in his room. She suspected he gazed more at the V8 than at her.

'Call me?' he yelled out hopefully.

'Maybe.' Kicking aside her sister's plastic Barbie-goes-Riding horse, Jade lifted the latch on her own white picket gate. A damp flying fur ball leapt into her arms.

'Oh, Marlon,' she murmured, kissing his neck, 'they want to see me again.'

'That you, Jadey?' A voice called urgently from the upstairs bathroom. 'I need you to help me unblock this toilet. Your brother's been putting toys down it again!' Sighing, Jade put down the Maltese terrier and disappeared into the gloom of 144 Federation Road.

niggling pain started to throb in her temple.

'I pay my board. And *his* petrol!' Jade could never bear to call her step-father by his name. 'Try to understand, Mum. Just because you've lived all your life in the suburbs, doesn't mean I have to. Have you considered I might make it as an actor?'

'Actor!' Margaret squeezed out a dishcloth as if she had Jade's neck in her hands. 'What kind of a life would that be? Out of work most of the time. How can you raise a family or buy a house without a proper job? No bank manager would ever give you a mortgage!'

'I don't want a mortgage.' Without noticing she was doing it, Jade slipped into an American accent and curled her lip like Heather Locklear in 'Melrose Place'. 'I ain't gonna hang around in this dump all my life. I'm gonna be somebody.' The moment the words slipped out, she regretted them.

'I see! Then there's no more to be said.' Her mother's voice was unnaturally high-pitched. 'I'll tell Grandpa you have a prior engagement.' She turned her back, poured some Ajax on the cloth and began rubbing the same places she'd just cleaned.

Jade longed to reach out and hug her, to take back the awful words. But it was impossible. They didn't have the kind of relationship where hugging and saying sorry ever happened. 'Can I give you a hand?'

'No.' The voice was brittle with tears. 'Almost finished.'

'You okay, Mum?' Samantha crept into the

19

kitchen, her hair stretched into glittery plastic bobbles, her smile pure suck-up. 'Fade, Jade,' she hissed, wrapping her scrawny arms around her mother's back.

Jade shot out of the room, stifling a howl of pain as she trod barefoot on a My Little Pony up-ended on the stairway. In her room, she gazed at the mirror, guilt stricken. She'd made her mother cry. 'Oh, Mum,' she whispered, 'I'll make you proud of me one day. I'll buy you front row seats for the Logie Awards, Samantha won't be allowed, and you'll see me getting 'Best Newcomer' and everyone clapping, then I'll slink up to the platform looking exquisite in . . . '

She jolted back to the present. *Oh, no! What will I wear on Saturday?* Panicked, she ripped open her wardrobe door and gazed at the miserable selection of Salvation Army bargains. The grunge look came naturally; all her money went on classes or the theatre. She had absolutely nothing to wear to meet someone like Daniel. She remembered pictures of him in the gossip magazines, a stunning model draped on his arm, her tiny heart-shaped face framed with jet-black curls. He'll hate me, she thought gloomily. I'm just plain big. I've never worn anything but boots and T-shirts in my life. And I'd look ridiculous painted up as a try-hard soapie chick.

The next day, after clearing away the lunch tables and setting up for the evening staff, she approached Giorgio.

'Just a small advance, say $250? It's the most important thing, it means the world to me and I'll love you forever.'

'What's this important thing? Giorgio looked up balefully from his cappuccino, unimpressed by the pleading girl kneeling at his feet. He'd known Jade for years. He'd seen her grow from a gawky schoolgirl into the answer to a red-blooded Greek's prayers, but she didn't fool him for a moment.

'Darling Giorgio, tomorrow is my grandpa's birthday. He'll be a hundred years old. I have to buy him something really special.'

'A hundred years old, that's something! I remember an old man in my village ...'

Jade controlled her impatience and fixed a 'gosh you are so wise and interesting' expression on her face as he rambled off on one of his interminable tales from Greece. But it worked. Pocketing the money at last, she kissed him hurriedly on the side of his leathery cheek and set off for Brunswick Street. There were some little boutiques there that had always enchanted her.

Friday afternoon shoppers crammed the narrow sidewalks as she made her way to her favourite, 'Primavera'. She dived into a doorway disguised by columns and a huge stone statue of Venus de Milo, and found herself face to face with Lee-Anne.

'Jade! What are you doing here? We sell dresses, you know.' Kohl-rimmed eyes travelled over the torn jeans and check shirt.

21

'I want the perfect dress to meet Daniel Hunter in!' She couldn't resist boasting. Lee-Anne, like a lot of girls at her school, had given her a hard time about her acting ambitions.

Lee-Anne's eyes widened. 'I see,' she waved purple nails at the clothes racks. 'It's terribly expensive here. Gigi designs everything herself.'

'I can afford it.' How annoying to have run into Lee-Anne of all people. 'Giorgio gave me an advance.'

'You've probably earned it,' she replied, cattily.

But Jade was having too much fun exploring the shop to feel offended. It had been decorated to look like a Tuscan villa, with wrought-iron racks, stone walls and huge oil paintings of vineyards. Candles flickered under burners of lavender oil. A glorious bowl of spiky delphiniums dazzled like an Italian summer sky.

'Wow, so beautiful,' she breathed.

'Are you here for the clothes, or the flowers? 'Cos I should warn you, there's nothing here under a couple of hundred bucks.' Lee-Anne scowled.

Jade ignored her, filling her arms with dresses, tops and skirts. It was hard to resist the classically designed silks and cottons. Jade loved simple unfussy clothes. These were perfect.

Lee-Anne interrupted her phone call to shout, 'The changing rooms are through there.'

Jade stripped and examined her body. She'd always thought herself too big. Her breasts were over-developed and her bottom was frankly an embarrassment. But her legs were not too bad; long, anyway. Better make the most of her assets. She slipped on a short silk dress.

'Fits you.' Lee-Anne poked her head round the door, chewing.

'My nipples show,' she peered anxiously in the mirror. She hated showing off too much of her body.

'It's the fashion. Look at Madonna.' Lee-Anne stared. 'You still with Wayne?'

'Depends what you mean by "with". How much is it?'

'Saw you with him last week in that ace car of his.' She carried on staring. 'Two hundred and forty-nine.'

'I'll take it.' It was worth it to see the expression on Lee-Anne's face.

Three days later, wearing her monstrously expensive dress, shoes borrowed from a girl at work and a huge smile she couldn't suppress, she arrived in town. The sky was a duck-egg blue and the streets were floodlit by late afternoon sunshine. Jade prowled along the pavement, ignoring the Italian restaurateurs vying for her attention and the hungry stares from gangs of bored teenagers. She was on the brink of something stupendous and she wanted to sing out for joy. Her legs felt like fast-growing stilts propelling her up; her hair, flying by her face, streamed out for miles around. Soon her body seemed to blend in with the whole universe. It was

23

the most amazing, ecstatic feeling. *I can do anything, I'm invincible!*

It was exactly three o'clock when she found herself in the waiting room of the three-storey limestone building in Thomas Street. There was no one in reception, but she knew she had the right address by the scene that greeted her. Ghastly parents playing 'my daughter's better than yours'. Finding a corner seat, well away from the other occupants, she pulled out the improving book she had lugged around for a year, *Strasberg On Method Acting*, and tried yet again to understand it. But the conversation from the other side of the room won.

'Has she done much work before?' That from a sad-looking, washed-out woman sitting beside a large man bursting with self importance.

'A few TV commercials. She was the girl who won all the money in the Lotto ad. Remember?'

Jade looked up with interest at the subject of their conversation. She'd seen the girl before at auditions. She was a plumpish strawberry blonde who usually wore too much make-up and was undoubtedly the source of the sickening aroma of cheap perfume.

'Don't fiddle with your hair!' the girl's mother hissed.

Jade couldn't understand why the girl didn't die of embarrassment. For once she was glad her mother stayed out of her life. Her mother might be desperately boring, but she had too much dignity to hang around auditions, scoring cheap points over other mothers.

At that moment the inner door opened and a stunning girl with miles of glossy chestnut hair strode out. She was wearing a slit skirt, boots and a cropped cardigan. Barely acknowledging her waiting parents, she marched, stony-faced, to the door. They jumped up dutifully and she heard the father's voice boom out, 'Sweetheart, did you get it?' as the door swung shut.

'Next?' A vibrant redhead in a wildly patterned sweater looked at Jade. It was Maggie Gold. They'd met before at the cattle call.

'Who are you?'

'Jade Silver, and we've met before.' She jumped up and held out her hand, taking the unwilling palm and pumping it vigorously.

Maggie looked annoyed.

'I'm next.' The bimbo jumped up breathlessly, tugging at the scrap of skirt that was failing to cover her bottom, and scuttled off after Maggie.

The mother, abandoned, stared at Jade. 'Is this your first audition?' She wanted Jade to distract her while she waited.

But Jade wouldn't answer. She was sitting bolt upright, breathing deeply, her mind focused and clear as a bell, consciously willing her heart to slow down. It seemed only minutes, although it was nearly thirty, before the bimbo was released. Jade stood up.

It was her turn.

3

'If I want your opinion, I'll ask for it,' the big woman in dungarees thundered at Daniel. She was rolling a camera perilously close to where he was sitting under an arc of powerful spots.

'I only suggested it might be a good idea to turn down the lighting.'

Jade stared at him, mesmerised. From her corner of the studio, shrouded in darkness, he looked like a Greek God, alone in the spotlights. Around her technicians prepared for the next audition, joking and wheeling their cameras around.

Maggie approached him. 'Darling, only one more to go.'

'It's pointless. The last one was a joke. Why don't you cast in Perth? At least the girls there have a decent tan.'

'Darling, we have to check the chemistry.' She

26

floated on, vodka and orange in one hand, bracelets jangling.

Daniel sighed. 'The chances of there being any chemistry under 2000 watts of light, saying lines from a script my dog could have written, is laughable!'

Jade's heart sank; he was clearly exhausted. *No wonder*, she thought, *hours of listening to people like those bimbos out there. But it will be different with me.* She tilted her chin confidently. *Just wait, Daniel Hunter.* He was raking his fingers now through blue-black hair, gleaming like a stallion's under the lights.

'Jade Silver!' Maggie called out from the intercom. 'On set please!'

Someone turned on the radio. Elaine Paige was singing the theme music from *Cats*. She took a deep breath, set her gaze firmly on his face and walked slowly into the spotlight.

'Hello, I'm Jade,' she purred, her voice throaty and low as she offered a cool slim hand.

'Jade.' He stood up, holding her hand firmly in his and smiling down at her.

Christ!, she thought, taking one incredulous look into his eyes, then dropping her gaze. *He can't be real, he can't!* Such glossy coal black hair, such a wonderful, wide curving mouth. And his eyes! She was in serious danger of drowning if she looked too long.

'Sit down.' His voice was deeper and warmer than it sounded on TV. He pulled the stool over so that they sat together in a pool of white-hot light. 'Have you learnt your lines?'

Jade nodded, speechless.

'That's more than I've done. The Christmas Fairy,' he nodded towards Maggie, 'only gave me a script today, so you'll have to bear with me if I make a fool of myself.'

Jade stared. How could anyone so gorgeous ever make a fool of himself? She listened in awe as he told her about the program and the characters they were playing. But it was hard to concentrate. She was relieved, moments later, when Maggie interrupted him.

'Okay, same place, Danny.'

'The name's Daniel.' He put an arm round Jade, drawing her into the camera line.

'We're on camera two,' he whispered, smiling.

Jade's heart thumped so badly, she was convinced he would hear. Her first line came out a hoarse whisper. She coughed, excused herself and started again. After that it got better, mostly thanks to him. He was a supportive actor, someone who gives to the person they're playing against. He believed her lines, his emotions tuned into hers. A sense of gratitude flowed through her, loosening up her performance. He's been doing this all day, she thought, yet he's still working to make it easier for me. She murmured lines like, 'Jason, I care about you, more than I can say'. Gradually, she was overcome by the intensity of the scene. Her voice shook; she was slipping under his spell.

28

'Cut!' Maggie announced cheerfully. She rushed over, jingling gold and clinking glasses. 'Darlings, febulous, febulous, febulous! Jade, we'll let you know.' Then she turned adoringly to Daniel. 'How about a bit of a drink? You've got an hour before the car comes.'

'Thanks, no.' He turned to Jade. 'Have you got transport?'

Jade smiled, wondering if he could hear the ocean rush of her blood. He terrified her, or maybe she terrified herself. She certainly couldn't trust herself to act cool around him. And she had far too much pride to be another groupie. In any case it was obvious that Maggie, who had the final say on casting, wanted to get rid of her. Not trusting her voice, she shook her head and strode out of the room without a backward glance.

In the street, her legs buckled. Holding on to the wall, she gasped for breath. The afternoon seemed extra bright, a brilliant sunset turning the street into a disco. Streaks of fuchsia lit up the violet sky. Scarlet spangles glittered from car bumpers and shop windows. Jade breathed in the city smells of dust, coffee, petrol and perfume, growing calmer.

It had gone well, brilliantly well. But she'd been to auditions before where she was convinced the part was hers, only to find a rejection in the mail. This was no everyday audition. 'Sunshine Coast' was the leading show in Australia, as well as having a huge following in the UK and Europe.

For Maggie, casting the role of Kerry would be a major decision. And she hadn't seemed too impressed. At the end of the day, her ability to act wasn't the point. It was whether her face would fit.

Daniel was a different matter. There was no mistaking the look in his eyes. Or was that just acting? Or perhaps he was a professional sleaze. She felt weak all over again thinking about it. A shop assistant peered anxiously out of a doorway.

'Are you okay?'

'Never better.' Jade straightened up and headed towards the station. She didn't know what would be more thrilling, working with Daniel or being a TV star. Or both, she laughed out loud. I want both, she shouted, running wildly down the ramp towards the train.

Her heart was still beating double time half an hour later as the Borringup train slid past the endless red-brick suburbs. All she could think of was the audition and Daniel. Her skin tingled where his fingers had touched, his voice echoed in her ear. Someone had left a newspaper on the seat next to her, and she found herself flicking to the horoscope page to see what was in store. *Mars is in the ascendant and career changes are on the way. Leo man will enter your life and steal your heart.* She wondered if Daniel was a Leo, then discovered she had been reading Wayne's star sign by mistake. Her own horoscope said nothing interesting, so she forgot astrology and decided to fill in her diary. When it came to describing the audition, she wrote

'I love Daniel Hunter', then signed 'Jade Hunter' over and over again to get the signature flowing properly.

By the time she trudged into the house, her elation was evaporating. She could hear Wayne's father, Alf, in the kitchen laughing with her step-father. They were close friends.

'Is that Meryl Streep home?' Her step-father had been drinking heavily. His face was flushed and his watery eyes looked belligerent.

Alf grinned inanely. 'Wow, what a knockout. Where have you been?' He was trying not to look at her legs.

'An audition. How was the birthday party?' She was supposed to call her step-father Dad, but managed to avoid it.

'Bloody awful!' he snapped. 'Not a drink to be had. Your aunt and your mother fussed round the old bugger. He looked as though he'd rather be in bed watching "Home and Away". And your brothers were out of control as usual. You should have been there to look after them.' There was a dangerous edge to his voice.

'Don't worry, love, if the part falls through.' Alf carried on oblivious. 'I've got a job for you. Me and the boys are thinking of doing a new advertising campaign with the giant Gorilla on the showroom roof. We'll have a gorgeous girl wriggling in its hand, like King Kong. And we thought we could do a press and TV campaign with you saying, *Help, I need a special deal Gorilla four-*

wheel drive to escape! What do you think?'

Jade looked up in amazement from the cup of tea she was making. 'You're not serious?'

Alf beamed with pleasure. 'Dead cert! And we think you would be perfect!'

Jade fought hard to control her reaction. She knew he thought he was doing her a favour. 'It's a great offer, Alf, but I don't think I'll be able to . . . '

'What!' The volcano blew. 'You won't be able,' her step-father mimicked. 'Yes, you bloody *will* be able. You'll do whatever Alf wants. It's the least you could do to repay me for the years I've had to put up with you in my house. Where are you going?'

'To bed.' Jade made for the door. When he started on that subject after a few beers, he could lose control. Once, in the winter, he kicked her out of the house and she'd had to sleep in the outside dunny.

'You can't go to bed,' he roared, 'your Mum and I want a night out on our own. You're baby-sitting.' He reached for another can.

'And Wayne'll be round to keep you company!' Alf chipped in, trying to change the subject. 'He's just put his new engine in.'

Jade felt like screaming. 'Sunshine Coast' was on later, and she wanted to watch without any inter-ruptions, particularly from Wayne droning on about the Commodore. She wanted to be alone to re-live every moment of the audition, particularly the exquisite touch of Daniel's lips on hers during the love scene. She wanted to melt all over again as she did when he spoke his lines. What were they? *Kerry, you're the most important thing in my life. Those other girls mean nothing now that I've found you* ... Corny lines, but he made them sound, well, powerful.

'Did you hear what I said?' Her step-father's face was puce. 'Oh, hello Princess!' He diverted his gaze to the door, where Samantha had sidled in wearing a minx-like expression. 'Sam-Sam, you'll get your old Dad a beer out of the fridge, won't you? Your sister's blanked out again. Alf, I swear that girl's schizo.'

Jade flashed him a look of pure loathing and was about to escape when her mother appeared. 'Oh, you're back. Good! Can you make supper for the kids tonight? We've decided to eat out at the Chinese.'

Samantha, who had delivered the beer with a winsome smile, was now fishing around in Jade's bag, on her usual search for Jade's diary.

'Get the hell out of there!' Jade yelled. 'That's private!'

'Don't swear.' Her mother looked up sharply, pulling on a pair of bright yellow rubber gloves.

'That wasn't swearing!'

'Bloody was,' bellowed her step-father, wiping the froth off his upper lip. 'I don't want my Samantha picking up your daughter's bad habits,' he growled at her mother, then turned back to Jade. 'You'd better smarten up, madam, or ... '

'Or what!' Jade snapped. She could put up with abuse herself, she'd long since stopped listening to anything he said, but when he attacked her mother, her blood boiled. She threw herself into the ensuing fight on automatic pilot. They'd said the same things to each other so many times, she often wondered why they bothered. He reminded her yet again how lucky she was to have a home, and how he took her in when her own father abandoned her. And how she ought to be more grateful and do more at home instead of hanging around the theatre with poofs. Living in a dream world, he yelled, big ideas! What makes you think you're so special? At least this time he didn't get violent.

Later, when the dust settled, she picked up Marlon who was cowering under the table, and retreated to her room. Throwing herself onto the bed, cuddling Marlon, she felt his tiny pink tongue lap her cheek.

'What if he's right,' she whispered shakily, 'and I'm fantasising about my life? I'm still only one of dozens up for this part.' It was too depressing to think about. Marlon's tawny eyes, fringed with white fur, filled with loving sympathy. She clutched him tightly for a moment.

The door burst open and her twin brothers rolled in, fighting.

'Yuk, kissing dogs.'

'Out,' she roared, leaping off the bed to slam the door after them. Slipping out of her beautiful dress, she hung it carefully in her wardrobe, where it shimmered in the dark like a priceless jewel. He'd touched it when he put his arm round her. If nothing else happens, she thought, stroking the silk, I'll have had one perfect day.

Tugging on her jeans, she noticed they were slack. Since this whole 'Sunshine Coast' business had begun she'd hardly eaten anything. Food made her feel sick. Now her jeans were too baggy. But it didn't matter, there was no one to see. Wayne didn't count. Feeling suddenly tearful, she scraped back her hair into a scrunchy and smeared her face with cleansing milk. Then she soaked a tissue in avocado eye cleanser and took off layers of mascara. An old Beatles song played on the radio. *She's leaving home, bye bye.* One day, she sighed. Why was it all her confidence seemed to evaporate when her step-father was around? He made her feel so useless. Why did her mother put up with it all?

An old photo album lay on her dressing-table. It seemed on every page there was a picture of her mother in an apron or with a cloth in her hand. This place is like the Sydney Harbour Bridge to her. As soon as she cleans everything, she starts at the beginning again. She searched the pictures for clues to her mother's life. But there were only baby and house pictures. There were pictures of her step-father in his workshop, like Wayne. What was it about men and cars? Even in their wedding album, the car seemed to dominate. But there were none of her real father. Her mother said he was from

35

Iceland, a merchant seaman. Sometimes she dreamed of him. He appeared to her against a wall of snow, like a blond giant. But when she reached out to him, she discovered he was made of ice, like one of those carvings in the Chinese restaurants.

She turned the page to the wedding picture. She saw herself, a tiny bridesmaid squinting into the camera, clutching the hem of her mother's dress. Her mother smiling anxiously at her step-father. How much slimmer she was then. Was it unhappiness that made her fat, or boredom?

On the next page there was a black and white studio portrait of her mother at eighteen. She looked like a hippie. Dark hair parted in the middle, dreamy expression, some sort of Indian caftan with little mirrors sewn on, her eyes sooty with mascara. She looked so innocent and gentle. Sweet, that was the word. But weak as well. No wonder she got nowhere. If there was one thing Jade had learnt, it was the importance of being strong. She held up her mother's picture to the mirror so that she could compare their faces. So alike in many ways. Yet Jade's face was stronger, her eyes more focused. Poor Mum, she thought, shoving the photo back into the album. Married to him, four kids and a quarter-acre block in Borringup. That's what happens if you give up on your dreams.

The front doorbell chimed.

'Jay-jay, Wayne's here.' Samantha poked her head round the door, cheeks smeared in blackberry jam.

'Come here, Sammy.'

'No. You'll hit me.'

'You deserve it, but I won't.' Jade tissued off Sam's face with her expensive Clarins. Her hair smelled of baby soap. She felt an uncharacteristic surge of affection.

'You've got hairs up your nose,' Sam lisped, eyes round with pleasure at the attention. 'Do you still love me?'

'Sure, but stay away from my diary, or I'll chop you up into bite-sized pieces and feed you to Alf's gorilla.'

'Can we have a bottle of Sharmonay for tea?'

'Don't be ridiculous. And get out of my wardrobe.'

'I saw your nipplies in that dress.'

'You're disgusting. Go and tell Wayne I'm coming.' Jade watched the skinny legs disappearing round the door, and her voice shrieking out to Wayne, 'Jade's nipplies are brown'. So like me at that age, she thought. Wild! How will she escape? Maybe she won't want to. Perhaps there's something wrong with me that I can't settle down with Wayne. After all, he'll be well-off one day, I can wrap him round my little finger, and he's actually quite good looking. She heard the hiss of more beer cans as Wayne settled in with the men and felt a rush of irritation. That is if you like red-haired, footy-playing car salesmen!

They were still drinking beer in the kitchen when 'Sunshine Coast' began. Her mother was agitating to leave. She was wearing her going-out clothes, a recycled designer dress in the same shade of brown as her house-cleaning tracksuit.

Her plaintive voice drifted in from the kitchen. 'Please don't drink any more. I'm starving, come on, let's go. We'll leave these lovebirds alone.'

'Patience, woman. Just finishing my beer,' he burped. 'Help yourself, Wayne.'

Jade found the headset, plugged out her family and sank gratefully into the title music of 'Sunshine Coast', straining to see Daniel in the opening sequences. She pictured her own name flashing on the screen. *Also starring Jade Silver as Kerry . . .*

'Jade.' Her mother pulled off her headset. 'Why did you take off that pretty dress? Wayne's in the kitchen. Quickly, nip upstairs and change.' She spoke in a stage whisper louder than most people's normal voices.

'Why? The last thing I want is Wayne getting ideas.' She watched her mother's puzzled face retreating, then replaced the headset. Daniel's ravishing face filled the screen.

'Hi, Kitten!' Wayne twanged out one of her earpieces, pulling some hair painfully at the same time.

'Get lost!' she screeched, more furiously than necessary. Then seeing the hurt expression on his face, added 'Let me wind down with a bit of TV, then I'll make supper.'

For the next thirty minutes she sat entranced. Not even the sight of Samantha, covered in lipstick obviously pinched from her drawer, distracted her. She focused on Scarlett Stone playing a bitch, Belinda the goody-two-shoes and of course her darling Daniel, so gorgeous she thought she would faint looking at him. *I'm as good an actress as any of them*, she thought. *Scarlett over-plays, and Belinda has a speech defect which is supposed to be cute but really sounds ridiculous. Oh please God, let me get this part. I'll work so hard, I'll never be nasty to my mother or beat up Samantha or fight with my step-father ever again.* The thrilling title music, wild above the crashing waves, faded.

Jade threw down the *TV Times*.

'She's choice!' Wayne gurgled with appreciation.

The front cover showed Scarlett posing seductively, her leopard body-stocking cut so low, you could see a hint of crimson lace from her bra. The headline read, 'Australia's Hottest Babe'. Jade suddenly felt depressed. She couldn't compete with that sort of display. She hated the whole idea of showing her body. They'd never cast her if it was 'Hot Babes' they wanted. Not to mention Daniel. No doubt he gets sucked in as much as Wayne, she thought. Men can be so stupid. A black cloud settled over her. All her lovely fantasies suddenly seemed hopelessly unreal.

The next day, and the day after that, Jade went round in a daze. At the restaurant she dropped a scalding tortellini on a customer, one of Giorgio's many mistresses. It's amazing what some women will do for free pasta, she thought, watching Giorgio patting over her legs with a clean cloth. He was puce with anger, but the old dear seemed to be enjoying the attention, so she got off lightly. But it wasn't so easy to get out of the Gorilla Girl ads. Wayne called her at work.

'They've got a brilliant ad campaign worked out. You'll be needed on Wednesday for the shoot at the car yards.'

'I'm not sure, er ... I may be at work.'

'Tell Giorgio to shove it. Better still, put him on to me, I'll tell him.'

'I can't talk right now – customers – got to go ...'

'Wait, please, Jade! You'll be terrific. It'll raise your profile in Borringup. Dad'll be so disappointed if you say no.'

How on earth could she explain to him? It was bad enough walking into supermarkets and delis and coming face to face with life-sized cardboard cut-outs of herself grinning inanely and pointing to a carton of milk. But to be seen wriggling like the bimbo in King Kong! Putting on her softest, sexiest, voice, she purred into the phone, 'Wayne darling, I can't do it. I have my career as an actress to think about.'

'You think you're too good for Gorilla Motors, don't you? Now that you've had a sniff of the big time we're not enough for you. Well, we don't need you.' Then he added nastily, 'Forget it. I'll get a *real* model from the agency'.

Jade sighed. She could imagine the scenes at home when Alf told her step-father. 'Okay, I'll do it. Now buzz off.' She slammed down the phone, furious with herself for weakening and furious with Wayne for making her feel bad. He was right though. She did think she was too good for stupid gorilla ads. But what was so wrong with being ambitious?

By the end of the week she could contain her nerves no longer. With shaking fingers she dialled her agent begging him to call 'Sunshine Coast'.

'It'll weaken your bargaining position if you look too eager!'

'Eager, schmeager, I gotta get the job,' she drawled in her best New York accent, then hung up before he talked her out of it.

'She was ebsolutely febulous!' Maggie grinned broadly at Marshall, the Executive Producer of 'Sunshine Coast'. 'No contest.'

'I'm worried about their colouring.' Marshall had the pause button on Jade's screen test, frozen at the kiss. 'She's got the whitest hair I've ever seen. Sure she's not an albino?'

'The light check must have been poor. That isn't true colour.' Maggie waved a tinkling arm at the screen 'She's a pale blonde with a cream skin. Her face bones are excellent and with her lack of colouring, Make-Up will be able to paint any look

41

we want. She reminds me of a white Persian cat.'

'Will she have claws enough to deal with Daniel?'

'Hard to say; looks as though she's had a tough time. No stage mother, and her agent was very surprised we'd picked her for call-back. I'd say she'd have to be a fighter to get this far. Put me in my place when I forgot her name.'

'She looks like Kerry, the Avenging Angel. Tall too. What did Daniel think?'

'You know Danny. His brain stopped the minute she walked in. There was so much chemistry we thought they'd spontaneously combust.'

'How much does she want?'

Maggie giggled, a low throaty chuckle as she lit up her thirteenth cigarette that morning. 'She's done nothing much. Theatre work, got a marvellous trained voice. Her agent has been crawling on the phone already. I'm sure they'll accept award rates.'

'Okay, you get her on a three-year contract, no options, basic salary. We can always can her if she doesn't work out.'

Maggie shuffled her papers, pleased. It was a good decision.

'Febulous! I'll wait a couple of days. Put up the gratitude level.'

Left alone, Marshall ran back the tapes, paying special attention to Jade's close-ups. Quite an extraordinary-looking girl. That hair, like some Nordic ice-maiden. A very strong face and determined jaw. Looked like she'd have no trouble handling Danny Boy. He'd been cutting a swathe through the female cast members. They'd lost a few good girls recently breaking contract or getting homesick. That was the trouble with teenage girls. No staying power.

A wave of indigestion gripped his stomach. Marshall reached for his pills.

4

It was Saturday morning, exactly one week since the audition and Jade was beginning to lose hope. Her moods had been see-sawing from suicidal despair to utter ecstasy. The butterflies in her stomach had grown into dragons. She'd eaten nothing and was sure her hip bones were tearing out of her jeans. At the restaurant, she jumped every time the phone rang.

'There are a couple of your mates out there,' Giorgio growled at Jade. 'Don't be all day gossiping!'

She peeped through the ficus plants. Sharon and Lee-Anne! Some friends! Ever since school, those two had given her a hard time. Once they'd shared school, lunches, homework, even boy-friends. But these days she couldn't get through to them. Perhaps it had something to do with Wayne. Lee-Anne acted so cool around him, it was suspiciously like a crush.

'Hi, what are you guys doing here?'

They were dressed to the nines in the depressingly common way that passed for sexy in Borringup. Wayne would have approved.

'We've come to talk to you.' Lee-Anne's cyclamen-lipsticked mouth was pursed in disapproval. 'Can you sit down for a while? It's very important.'

'Jadey,' Sharon began seriously, fluffing up her fringe, 'we're very worried about you. Aren't we, Lee-Anne?'

'We've been talking to everybody, and we all agree it's time you knew the truth.'

'The truth about what?' Jade looked into their heavily made-up eyes. One of them, or maybe both, had been dipped in Dior's 'Poison'.

'Wake up to yourself ... ' Sharon began.

'You're living in a fantasy land ... '

'What the hell are you talking about?' Jade felt her temper rising.

'All this acting nonsense. Wanting to be a star!'

'You're nearly nineteen. Isn't it time you gave up such childishness?'

It was the fake concern that really infuriated Jade.

'You're jealous, aren't you? It's Wayne. Lee-Anne, you've always been after him!'

'Of course not,' she pouted back indignantly. 'I just feel sorry for him. Have you any idea how upset he is? And now you're pretending to have a date with Daniel Hunter, and buying dresses to meet him in!'

'We think you're going mad,' Sharon chirped.

Lee-Anne's face was purple with moral right-eousness. 'What has Wayne done to deserve this? He's been loyal to you all your life. How could you make such a fuss about helping him with his new ad campaign? You're lucky to get any work! What kind of a bitch are you?'

'The kind of bitch who does this,' and without thinking Jade yanked the pristine linen cloth, set for dinner with silverware, water jug, glasses and a small bowl of pansies, into their horrified faces. Lee-Anne's mouth made a bright pink 'O' as it dis-appeared under the table. Their screams mingled with smashing glass and brought Giorgio running from the bedroom upstairs where he was 'advising' the new waitress he'd just hired.

Sharon stumbled up shakily, a pansy dripping over her forehead. 'She is mad, Samantha was right!' She was chalk white under the tan make-up.

Lee-Anne crawled around the floor looking for her bag. Her skirt rucked up to her waist and revealed a red satin Barbarella G-string, which tem-porarily diverted Giorgio. She was whimpering like a sick puppy. 'Oh, oh, oh.'

Jade started to escape, but Giorgio had her firmly by the elbow.

'Did you do this?'

'Yes.'

'You're fired!'

'Good.'

It wasn't until she reached the train station that it hit her. No job, no friends, no money, no boyfriend; she'd never trust that sneaky bastard again. And as for Samantha! But these were tiny pinpricks compared to the pain of being so close and yet so far. Oh, why hadn't she heard from her agent?

Inside the station, a drinks booth was signposted by a life-sized cardboard cut-out of Miss Dairy Queen pointing to the cooling fridge, saying 'Rich, creamy milk, all you'll ever want.'

Grab a life, thought Jade, hurrying past in case anyone noticed who she was.

That night, after peeling the potatoes and vacuuming all the carpets, she escaped to her room. She couldn't face the little traitor Samantha who'd obviously been gossiping to Sharon and Lee-Anne. *Probably broadcast my diary at school for years,* she thought murderously. How many other people were laughing behind her back? Miss Dairy Queen, Borringup's biggest cardboard cut-out!

Flinging herself on her bed, she reached for the Strasberg book. The open window let in a gold, late-afternoon glow, warming her body. For a while she tried to bury her pain in learning. But her eyes felt heavy and the drowsy smell of wallflowers drifted in and out, just as thoughts of Daniel drifted around her mind.

Somewhere a telephone shrieked, dragging her back to consciousness.

'Jade, are you there?'

'Is it for me?' Jade was halfway down the stairs, heart thumping.

'It's that man from your agency.' Jade's mother handed over the phone, holding it away from her as if it was infectious.

Jade grabbed it. 'Yes?' she almost screamed.

'You got it!'

Jade had the presence of mind to place the phone carefully onto the polished fake antique table, before she let out a blood-curdling scream. Several minutes later, hyperventilating from jumping on the spot and whooping with delight, she picked it up again. 'When, where, why . . . '

'Don't you want to know how much?'

'I'd do it for nothing, as long as I get it!'

'Jade, are you sure this is what you really want? I mean it's hardly theatre, it's a mainstream, popular soap. You may never get a good film role if people see you as a soapie actor.'

'Sign me up! It's what I want.'

'You'll just be a celebrity and your looks could go against you. Please be sensible. You've always struck me as a serious actress . . . '

'What do you mean "my looks could go against me"?'

'Well. You have a natural beauty. They'll change your image.'

'I won't change. Sign me up. I'll be working with Daniel Hunter, and my face will be in *Dolly*. This is the happiest day of my life!' Jade was too dizzy with joy to notice the look in her mother's eyes.

'Congratulations, Jade. You've really done it.' Her mother summoned a smile and wiped her hands on her apron awkwardly.

Samantha looked up from her crayoning with a winsome smile. 'Mum, can I have Jay-jay's bed?'

For once, Jade didn't feel the slightest bit annoyed at her sister's manipulations. Quite the reverse. Grabbing her hand, she danced her upstairs. 'Come on, Sammy,' she cried, brimming with love, 'I'll give you my *TV Times* poster collection. In fact, I don't think there's anything I want to take. I'm starting a new life! I'm going to be one of *them*. You'll be collecting posters of me soon!' she exulted, letting out another ear-splitting whoop of joy.

'Sydney ahead, and the skies are clear. It's a beautiful spring day. We'll be touching down in twenty minutes.' The intercom crackled off.

Jade stretched luxuriously, a huge smile spreading over her face. The sky outside, a brilliant sailor blue, looked as if it had been airbrushed on to the window. On a neat plastic tray in front were the remains of lunch. Like a doll's party, she thought, miniature jams, cheese, salt and pepper. How Sam would have loved them. She suppressed a wave of guilt. Everyone had turned up at the airport to see her off. So embarrassing!

Her mother had given her a gold compact. It had been a present from her own father, the only thing that remained of him. Jade clutched it tightly in her hand. Wayne gave her a miniature silver Commodore on a chain and a soppy look. Samantha gave her a scrawly love letter and had to be peeled away sobbing. The twins disappeared and were found later riding on the baggage roundabout. Her step-father shook her hand and gave her the name of his accountant. She noticed respect in his eyes for the first time. But it was her mother's face she wanted to forget. The pain in her eyes was unbearable.

She pulled out her Strasberg book – might as well do something constructive – but the words swam in front of her eyes. Taking out her compact mirror, she noticed her cheekbones looked more pronounced. Thank God she'd lost those extra kilos waiting for the audition results. She was wearing her jade green dress. Most of her old clothes had been put in the garbage, then pulled out again by Sam. She could picture the silly Miss Dairy Queen costume in Sam's playbox, where it belonged.

There was a soft velvet pad in the compact. She stroked it gently over her cheeks and forehead. It was soothing. The sweet powdery smell reminded her of her mother. Tears pricked the back of her eyes. How would she cope without Jade? At least when she was around her mother had an ally when he lost control. She snapped the case shut, suddenly furious. All those years he'd laughed at her and put her down. Things were very different now. Last night she overheard him boasting to Alf about his 'daughter' hitting the big time. The hypocrite!

Closing her eyes, she floated off into a day-dream of the future. Then Daniel appeared again. This time she didn't resist.

Landing at Sydney, she half expected him to be waiting.

'Are you Miss Silver?' A man, bearing a frightening resemblance to Wayne, interrupted her fantasy. 'I've come to collect you, courtesy of Channel 6. Is this all your luggage?' He led her outside to a taxi and on in a terrifying rush through the streets of Mascot, Woollahra and Darlinghurst. The sky was turning amethyst, lit by the brilliant jewels of a thousand neon signs. The chill evening air smelt of exotic restaurants and garbage. Jade felt excitement blowing up like a balloon in her chest. When they stopped outside the marble splendour of a luxury apartment block and the driver told her this was Paradise Towers, she thought she might burst.

Her contract gave her free luxury accommodation for one month until she either took it on herself, or found somewhere cheaper to stay. I'll take it on, she murmured, undulating perfectly across the Italian mosaic lobby under a chandelier of topaz glass and wrought iron. A huge black man in an evening suit and gold bow tie greeted her warmly. The label on his lapel read 'Ben'.

'Here's your key, Miss Silver. Your key to Paradise.' His deep West Indian laugh followed her as she stepped into the lift.

It was an open lift, like a golden bubble of glass, floating up the wall of apartments. At the seventh floor, it whispered to a halt. Glass partitions slid apart to reveal a deep cream carpet stretching like snow ahead of her. She couldn't hear her own footsteps as she moved towards number seventy-seven and fitted the ornate gold key into the lock.

Inside was a sight that took her breath away. Losing her cool completely, she kicked off her shoes and screamed with excitement like a child on Christmas morning. For there, spread out in the dying indigo light, was the whole magnificent city. From the Harbour Bridge like a Lego toy, to the swooping pink shells of the Opera House, reflecting the setting sun. The sky, a velvety lavender, wrapped around the apartment, every room slashed open to the city. Jade rushed around, exclaiming out loud at the exquisite powder-blue sofas and antique white walls, broken up by vast mirrors flickering back the city lights. She felt like Alice in a sophisticated Wondercity. The phone rang. Stumbling for a light switch, she found an ivory phone at least double the normal size. Perhaps I am Alice, she giggled to herself, and I'm shrinking.

'Jade? Everything okay?' It was her agent, a new note of respect in his voice. 'Your scripts for next week should have been delivered, and a small thing from all of us here at Players. And a word of advice, Jade, don't let fame go to your head, it's a very temporary . . .'

But Jade wasn't listening. Under the bright halogen lights, she spotted a basket of orchids as big as the table they were sitting on. And beyond them another huge bouquet of sherbet-coloured roses, shimmering in gold paper. A delicate bunch of freesias shrank beside them. In the bedroom, there was an even larger display of delphiniums, as blue as the Mediterranean.

She discovered the freesias were from her mother, and the orchids from Channel 6; her agent had sent the roses. But the delphiniums, startlingly blue against the soft primrose-yellow furnishings, had no card. Her heart leapt wildly. Daniel must have sent them.

The phone rang again. Daniel? Tripping over an ornate side table she hurled herself at the phone.

'Hi, mate. It's me, Wayne,' he said in his usual nasal drawl. 'Guess what?'

Her heart sank, then hardened with irritation. 'I expect you've got car trouble. How did you get my number?'

'From your Mum. Did she tell you about the fanbelt?' Wayne sounded surprised.

'No, and I can't talk, I'm expecting a call.' She put the phone down quickly. *You idiot*, she thought, *why would Daniel call me*? He'd only met her at an audition, it meant nothing. And here she was building it up into something significant. *This won't do, Jade*, she told herself firmly. *You are here to make a name for yourself, not to get caught up in a schoolgirl crush over someone as glamorous as Daniel Hunter.*

She carried on exploring. The kitchen was brilliant. Not a finger-painting in sight, just miles of gleaming stainless steel and peacock-blue marble.

There was a fun microwave that played a pinging tune and lit up like the control panels of a DC10, and a huge blender that hummed satisfactorily when she pressed the 'shredding' button. Once they were going she let the dishwasher join in, then the sink grinder. My own reggae band, she laughed out loud, hip-hopping on the black marble tiles. In the fridge she found a bowl of exotic fruit and a bottle of champagne labelled 'Welcome to Paradise Towers'.

Stuffing a whole apricot into her mouth, she popped open the champagne, found an elegant glass and set off towards the sunken jacuzzi. The bathroom was pristine. Soft peach towels, bottles of rose geranium bubbles and water jets. Soon the jacuzzi was boiling like a geyser, champagne and rose bubbles mixing on the marble slabs.

This is heaven, she sighed, singing as much of 'Material Girl' as she could remember, as loudly as possible. Languidly she reached for the champagne, but to her surprise it tasted disgusting. I'll have to get used to it, she thought happily. Everyone drinks champagne.

Outside the sky had turned midnight blue and the city lights were close enough to touch, like the fairy lights on her own Christmas tree. She had that wonderful big feeling again, as if she was part of the city and it was part of her.

The Plan is working, she gloated. Four years ahead of time. From now on, I'm going straight to the top. No more promotions, no more ads.

I've arrived!

5

Daniel Hunter was the first person she set eyes on the next morning when she arrived at the studios. A taxi picked her up at six o'clock, but she'd been ready an hour before that. He was standing in the lobby, surrounded by adoring girls who all looked as though they'd been up since four o'clock conditioning and blow-drying their hair. She'd never seen so much make-up and such short skirts in her life. Beside them, Lee-Anne would have looked like a computer nerd. He glanced up as she came in.

'Jade! Welcome.'

The girls weren't nearly so pleased to see her, scrutinising every aspect of her clothes, face and hair. They looked disappointed.

'Meet our production assistant, and Felicity from make-up, and these three,' he indicated a trio of girls with skirts like postage stamps, 'are from admin.'

'Hi!' Jade summoned up a warm smile. Difficult in the face of such overwhelming lack of interest. They turned their backs and carried on gossiping.

'Time to get started!' Daniel extracted himself and put a protective arm around her shoulder. 'Let me take you through to the studios. You'll be wanted in the main office, I expect. ' He steered her firmly towards a door marked 'Closed to the Public' and down a dimly-lit corridor. 'I'll take you in to say hi to a few others first. I know Scarlett is dying to meet you. She's been asking questions about you all week. And Belinda was watching your audition tapes in the Green Room the other day. By the way, you were brilliant in audition. The producers are thrilled.'

She felt his smile again. It affected her physically, like standing by a roaring fire. Belinda and Scarlett were in the Green Room running through some lines together. Scarlett was wearing her trademark red clothes, a tight crimson shift dress with matching lipstick and nail polish. Belinda wore a fluffy white Angora sweater, despite the heat, and baby pink tights. It was Belinda who jumped up eagerly.

'Jade, gweat, you've awwived!' She flung her arms around Jade's neck, tickling her skin. The smell of 'Anais Anais' was overpowering.

'Congratulations on your first part.' Scarlett uncoiled herself from her beanbag and stood up. 'Must be quite a thrill for you!'

56

'Don't listen to her.' Belinda stuck her tongue out at Scarlett. 'She's just jealous because you'll be playing love scenes with Daniel. Lucky you,' she added, giving Daniel the benefit of a wide gap-toothed smile.

'So, what have you done before?' Scarlett lifted one perfectly plucked eyebrow.

'Nothing much. Most of my experience has been in the theatre.' Jade felt dizzy. She wasn't intimidated by Scarlett, but it was hard to adjust to meeting these people in the flesh after watching them so long on television. As if she had entered her own dream and the real world was slipping away.

'So what made you decide to slum it in television?' she continued. 'Fancied yourself on the front cover of the *TV Times*?' She smiled sweetly.

'I'll come to you for advice on that. By the way, you looked fabulous in that leopard-skin body-suit last week,' Jade added, then turned to Daniel. 'It's cold in here; must be the air-conditioning.' She could hear the sharp intake of breath behind her, as they moved off to look for the producer.

Outside the door, Daniel laughed out loud. 'I've never seen anyone bring Scarlett to heel so quickly. She'll respect you for that. She may even retaliate, but don't worry. You'll be able to control her!' Then he plunged into the next office. 'Marshall, she's here. I thought you'd want to see her.' Then he winked at Jade and disappeared.

She found herself looking into the darkest, heaviest eyes she'd ever seen.

'Come in!' Marshall Hughes filled his vast leather chair, looking more like a retired colonel than the executive producer. He was washing down indigestion tablets with a large mug of black coffee. Jade had to peer over the wall of scripts, faxes and old copies of *Alliance* on his desk. 'Had a terrible night.' He burped. 'You look fresh! Daniel been showing you around?' His furry eyebrows met in the middle, frowning. 'I want to warn you about . . .'

The phone rang. It took him several minutes to find it in the debris. By the time he came up for air, Maggie appeared carrying two more coffees.

'Here you are, darl.' Her husky voice was aimed at Marshall. 'Sweetie pie!' Noticing Jade, a brilliant smile lit up her face. 'Gorgeous to see you again. Like the Towers? You'll have a ball there. Run along to make-up, Felicity's looking for you.'

Jade backed out, amazed at the difference in the way Maggie treated her. Through a glass panel she could see the set of the cafe in 'Sunshine Coast'. It looked smaller than it did on TV, and packed with activity. Cameras dwarfed the milk bar and technicians milled around, joking as they worked. She could feel the hum in the air. I'm part of all this she smiled, hugging herself. I'm really here at last.

'Jade. There you are.' The production assistant grinned, her good humour restored. 'Did he put the hard word on you?' She winked. One spiky plastic eyelash fell like a spider on her cheek.

'What do you mean?' But she knew she wasn't talking about Marshall.

'Dan the Man,' she giggled.

'He's been kind to me.'

'Yeah? I wonder why.' Winking again she turned and teetered off on impossibly high stilettos down the dim corridors, lit by flashing red signs, Studio On and Do Not Enter.

'Where are we going?' she asked the chiffon-draped bottom. It made her seasick watching.

'Make-up. And I've got your call sheets for tomorrow.' She turned round, her wide shiny mouth grinning. 'No scenes today. How do you feel?'

'Like the first day at school, thanks,' she admitted. 'A bit nervous, but wildly excited.'

'Atta-girl. So would I be if I was going to be kissing Danny boy every day and getting paid for it. We're laying bets in production he'll have you in his clutches by the end of the week.'

She remembered the pictures of him in the gossip mags with a gorgeous model. So he couldn't be trusted?

'He's so hot, he ought to carry a government health warning. No one's safe!' She giggled and wriggled at the same time, then pushed Jade through a purple swing door with 'Scarlett's Dressing-up Box' graffitied on the door.

'Hi, Felicity,' Jade began nervously.

Felicity grinned, happy her name had been remembered. 'Sorry I was a bit off before. Jealousy, darl. You chicks get paid humungous amounts to have a good time, comb your hair in front of the camera and swan around shopping centres being mobbed by fans. I have to work my guts out in make-up, I keep longer hours than you, and I get paid peanuts.'

'I hate make-up and I'd rather not be mobbed by fans.' She felt quite alarmed at the thought.

'Goes with the job, darl. You'll get to love it. I've seen them all come and go here. Sweet as pie when they arrive. Professional drama queens when they leave.' Felicity swept up her hair in a bandeau and attacked her face with a brush the size of a fist. 'D'ya remember Brooke Donovan?'

'Do I. She's the biggest thing ever.'

'I did her face for three years; I was closer to her than her mother. She went to the UK, hit the big time. Now she passes me on the street and looks at me like I'm dog droppings.'

Jade couldn't imagine her favourite actor doing that.

'Would you look at these cheekbones? You're going to be a piece of cake to do.'

For the next few hours she felt like a queen bee buzzed over by her workers. And the transformations were staggering. After every make-over, a polaroid photo was taken. Then Felicity started all over again, changing the shape of her eyes and mouth with an artist's palette of colours. Hot rollers and hair weaving created a mass of tumbling curls which was pinned up or let fall. Every so often, Daniel looked in to smile his encouragement.

'How's it going? Wow, what a babe!' Then he'd disappear, leaving her breathless.

It was so difficult to harden herself against him. At one o'clock, he walked in on a photo shoot where she was made up as Kerry, wearing a Studebaker white linen mini-dress, white high pumps and her hair piled up, a heavy fringe waving seductively down one side of her face.

'You look like pure cream,' he grinned. 'Can I drink you?'

'You can't touch her,' Felicity growled, fluffing blusher on Jade's cheeks. 'Clear off, Danny boy. If you're hungry, there's a gaggle of fresh fans in the street.'

'She's got to eat.' He took her hand firmly and led her out of the spotlight. 'I've booked a table at Latino's. For two.' He pushed past Felicity and led her towards the door.

'Be careful of her make-up,' she shouted.

'We're going to have lunch, not an affair.'

'Same thing where you're concerned!'

Jade's stomach churned. 'I thought I might skip lunch,' she began.

'Nonsense,' he countered. 'You need feeding up. And a little sunshine. I've got us an outside table.' He led her out to the street where a huge dusty Jaguar sat, half on the pavement. The head and one paw of a creamy golden Labrador lolled in the open window, chocolate-brown eyes cocked at the passing traffic.

'Meet Heroine,' he said proudly, opening the

door for Jade. Heroine thrust her nose into Jade's ear, her tongue lapping her hair.

She glanced back nervously as the wet nose tickled her ear again. Heroine was sitting on thousands of unopened letters heaped up on the back seat and spilling over on to the floor. There were pink love-hearts and scented stickers on some of them.

'Fan mail. We all get it. I keep meaning to answer them.' He revved up the engine and roared off down the street.

Jade waited for the usual enthusiastic description of the engine capacity. But he said, 'I've never seen her take to a stranger so quickly. Normally she sulks when I have friends.'

It dawned on her he was talking about the dog. 'Does she live in the car?'

'During the day. She hates to be left at home in case she misses something.' He squealed round a corner and lurched to a stop. Heroine and Jade were thrown forward.

A doorman leapt out from the shade of a fig tree to whisk open the doors. Daniel tossed him the keys and grabbed Jade's hand, while Heroine trotted dutifully after.

'Meester Hunter, this way.' A tall swarthy man with a high-gloss pony-tail bowed deeply and led them through a jungle of plants twinkling with fairy lights, onto a sunlit terrace. A ripple of excitement ran through the diners, heads swivelled, women pulled their shoulders back and arched their necks. For a moment the noisy chatter of well-bred voices died down, then rose again as they settled into a corner table.

'You're making quite a stir!' Daniel grinned appreciatively. 'Not surprising, made-up like that. Is that the final Kerry look?'

'Yes.'

'I heard they're going to try you under the sun lamps this week. With a tan, you'll look like a palomino.'

Jade felt a blush warming her cheeks. Would her foundation be able to disguise it? She buried her face in the table-sized menu.

'It's all in Italian,' she complained. 'And I only ever learnt French. Badly at that.'

'I can't imagine you doing anything badly.'

'I thought I could get by pretending to be Gerard Depardieu in *Green Card*. But my French teacher wanted me to learn irregular verbs.'

'And did you?'

'What I learnt was irregular. And it wasn't French either.'

Daniel laughed, a loud glad-to-be-alive sound that made a group of middle-aged women at the next table look round with interest.

'What was it?'

'That school couldn't help me go where I was going.'

'Where's that?'

Jade told him about the Plan. She couldn't hide her enthusiasm. Suddenly she realised she'd been babbling for over ten minutes and all he'd done was stare at her. 'Do you think I'll make it?' she asked, breathlessly.

He said, 'You handled Scarlett well. And you look gorgeous. You'll do well in television, if that's what you want.' He signalled to the waiter to take their order. 'What did you do before coming to Sydney?'

'Oh, er, some theatre . . .' Jade was relieved when the waiter appeared. She did *not* want to tell him about Miss Dairy Queen, or worse, the Gorilla Girl ads. 'I'll have a Caesar please, and the catch of the day with salad.'

The waiter couldn't take his eyes off Jade's long legs in the mini-dress. For the first time, she didn't feel offended. It was just a matter of believing herself to be Kerry. But she wished Daniel wouldn't stare. Across his shoulder a gilt mirror hung on the wall. She could see her reflection, and hardly recognised the striking stranger with high cheekbones, darkly drawn, almost mysterious eyes, and full lips glistening plum red, the colour startling against pale skin. Her nails, like blood-dipped talons, had been extended by the manicurist. They drilled nervously on the glass table.

'Don't worry, I won't make a pass at you.' His voice dropped to a husky whisper. 'Even though you are the most stunning girl I've seen in years.'

Jade flushed with heat. Was he suggesting she was one of his fans waiting for a word from the master? She touched her face; it was burning.

Please God, let the make-up be thick enough to hide her embarrassment.

'And for you, Meester Hunter?' The waiter coughed discreetly.

'I'll take the oysters and a double veal medallion. And three pork cassoulets for my dog. Oh, and a bottle of Moet.'

The waiter almost choked. 'I'm so very sorry, we cannot have the dog in the restaurant. The other diners . . .' He gave a Gallic shrug.

Heroine came out from under the table where she had been snoozing happily on Daniel's feet. She landed a heavy paw on the waiter's leg and cocked her head on one side.

'You wouldn't want to upset the lady, would you?' He motioned towards Jade. 'It's her dog and it pines if we leave it in the car. Terrible noise; put off all your customers!'

'Perhaps an exception then, just this once?' He gave Jade a longing look and scurried away with their order.

He lied so easily, she thought, watching him stroke Heroine. What is he really like under that layer of charm?

Then he looked up, grinning. 'I bought a new horse last month. An Anglo-Arab hunter. Pure white mane and tail; reminds me of you.'

She laughed in spite of herself. 'A horse?'

'Yes, beautiful body, unusual colouring, but too easily led. And she kicks.' His eyes glinted with meaning.

'Can I take a picture of you with my daughter?' A plump woman in a straw hat like a pancake interrupted, pushing a nervous teenager towards Daniel.

'What's your name?' he asked, drawing the girl forward and smiling at the camera. As the flash died, he withdrew a fan card from his pocket, scribbled 'for Emma' and smiled again at Pancake Hat.

'You'll be doing that soon. Everywhere you go, people interrupt. They think your character is a real person.'

'Isn't it terribly exciting to be famous?' Jade watched him flop back in his chair.

'Does the idea excite you?'

'It did, when I first got the part. I mean once you're well known, you can get better parts, have a real career. Otherwise you'd spend all your life as a wanna-be.'

'It's not that simple. We're all wanna-be's, all our lives. I warn you, fame doesn't solve anything.'

'My second warning today.' Jade looked chastened.

'Marshall?'

'Yes, but he was interrupted.' She watched him fill her glass with foaming champagne, the crystal goblet misting up instantly in the warm sun. Should she tell him she hated champagne? He'd think her unsophisticated. And he'd be right. She was a sham in this dress, a counterfeit, a con artist. Any moment now Giorgio will march in and order me back to the kitchen, she thought. Or the clock will strike twelve and I'll be revealed in ripped jeans and baggy shirt, my hair will straighten and my eyes will disappear into piggy little green blobs. Her nails drummed faster. Picking up the glass, she took a gulp and swallowed quickly, so that she wouldn't taste it.

'Probably wanted to warn you to stay away from me. I say, are you feeling all right? You've gone a funny colour.'

'I'm fine,' she heard herself say.

'Good. Well, drink up, this is over a hundred dollars a bottle.'

Nervously she glanced over his shoulder at the mirror again. Funny how confident she looked! Like watching an actress on a screen. Lifting the stem of her glass gracefully, she deliberately raised her chin, letting her lashes fall, lips parted in conscious imitation of Scarlett Stone. Then she sipped her champagne, replaced the glass and smiled seductively up at him from beneath her lashes. It was a series of manoeuvres she'd practised many times at home, in front of the mirror. Daniel leaned forward, an eager smile on his lips. Gosh, she thought, men are easily impressed. Even celebrities!

'Are you flirting with me?' he grinned.

How deflating! 'You wish.'

'Because that's my role. Or so everyone thinks. It won't just be Marshall warning you off me.'

She took another gulp of champagne to hide her embarrassment. 'Everyone's been warning me about you.'

'Have they scared you off?' His smile was teasing.

'Should I be?' Jade held his gaze. The champagne was definitely affecting her judgement, but it made her feel braver. She took another mouthful.

'I hope not.'

Now her heart was thumping unsteadily. Champagne bubbles burst behind her eyeballs.

'Because,' he continued 'I'd like you to think of me as a friend. TV is a strange world. Not every one is as they seem to be.' He reached across the table and imprisoned both her hands in his. 'If you get into trouble, you can always call me.'

She stared into his eyes, the only still points in a revolving room. Suddenly she felt dizzy. Then a tall red-head swam into view, wearing a black crocheted dress over nothing at all. She made for their table on what seemed to be a pair of stilts.

'Daniel darling, I see you've brought your girlfriend out for lunch.' She pointed to Heroine busy guzzling a bowl of meat that smelt fragrantly of oregano and garlic. 'And who is the Ice Princess? Not your usual type, darling.' She bent down over his chair to nibble his ear.

Jade froze, then snatched her hands away. How incredibly rude! She recognised the girl from a major drama series – she'd won a Logie for best actress.

'Sherrilyn, this is Jade Silver, the hottest up-and-coming star in television.'

Jade held out her hand. 'Sherrilyn who?' She smiled sweetly.

The girl flushed as red as her mane and hissed, 'Put a muzzle on her,' before teetering off on seven-inch heels.

'You do need a red ribbon,' said Daniel as he raised his glass to Jade.

Jade prudently put hers down. 'She was offensive.'

'I'm not arguing. You have to be tough to survive in this town. I'm impressed. Where did you learn unarmed combat?'

'At home.'

He frowned thoughtfully. 'You had a difficult time at home?'

His expression was sympathetic, but she wasn't fooled. She'd said enough for one day. 'It was okay. I left because I wanted more out of life than settling down with the boy next door and having babies. I'm ambitious.'

He pushed away his plate. 'Very ambitious?'

Jade fought a sudden urge to tell him all about the chaos at home, her step-father's abuse and drinking, her hopeless, Ajax-obsessed mother, the kids' toys and nappies everywhere, her years of loneliness, of feeling unwanted. But he wouldn't want to hear any of that. 'Yes,' she replied firmly, 'very ambitious.'

Suddenly the light went out of his eyes. 'I hope you find what you're looking for in Sydney,' he said coolly, then paused to sign his autograph on a Japanese girl's shirt. Two friends stood by giggling and clicking their cameras.

Jade noticed how patiently he spelled their names. The fountain pen shrank in his hand. Everything about him was big. His hands, his shoulders, the generous proportions of his mouth and eyes. Women, all women, seemed to behave differently near him. He's dangerous, she decided. He has everyone eating out of his hand. Even me! Her own hands shivered in her lap where he'd touched them.

'. . . next week. What do you think? Jade, have you been listening to me?'

'Pardon?'

'Sorry for boring you. Let's go. I'll drop you off at the studio – got a promo to shoot out of town.'

He left her at the main entrance, cheerfully blasting his horn before screeching off round the corner.

She watched him go, Heroine's ears flapping like an old airman's scarf, disappearing in a dust storm. The sun slid behind a cloud. Turning into the cool interior, she saw the red-head talking to some of the girls from wardrobe. They stopped when she walked in, then deliberately turned their backs. They'd been talking about her, she knew. Perhaps she'd overdone it; her tongue had always been too quick. Maybe the girl had reason to be bitchy to Daniel. *Who knows what trail of wreckage he's left behind over the years, how many hearts he's broken?* Then she overheard 'Didn't take her long to fall into line,' greeted by loud cackling. Shaking with rage, she dived into the lift. How absolutely unbearable to be the laughing-stock of

those spiteful girls. How pathetic to have suc-
cumbed to his charm so quickly.

She burned with shame.

Over the afternoon, she calmed down. She met
up with Belinda at rehearsals.

'Pay no attention to Sherrilyn,' she whispered.
'Everyone holds hands with Daniel at lunch. He's a
touchy sort of a guy. And she's a professional bitch.'

They sat in a circle, reading from their scripts,
discussing their roles. Jade felt she knew Kerry
already and the director congratulated her after the
rehearsals. Acting is acting, she decided, whether
it's in the theatre or in front of a video camera. She
enjoyed herself so much, she forgot the red-head.
But she couldn't forget Daniel.

There was no sign of him when she left. A
crowd of people stood around in the foyer waiting
for taxis. Then Belinda appeared at her side.

'Are you staying in Pawadise Towers?'

'Yes, my free month.' Jade was grateful for
Belinda's friendship.

'All that luxuwy is addictive. I found it hard
when I had to move out. I live with my gwandma
now.'

'I'm thinking of staying, whatever the cost.'

'You want to live in Pawadise all the time?'

Jade chuckled. 'I suppose so.'

'Beware of the serpent, then. Goodnight.' And
she was gone.

Jade watched the swing doors close. An odd
tight feeling crept into her throat.

6

That night Jade had a terrible dream. She was alone, swimming in an ocean of red liquid. It tasted sweet, so she drank it. The more she drank the more she wanted, until a heavy feeling of nausea overtook her. Desperate, she thrashed around looking for land, but the only thing she could see was a frozen glacier in the distance, melting in the midday sun. She woke up to find the blankets on the floor, her sheets twisted around her legs and her scalp damp with sweat.

Everything was unnaturally quiet. She waited for the twins to jump on her bed before realising she wasn't in Borringup. Then the phone rang.

'Jade? Scarlett here. We've got the same call times and I'm to pick you up at six.'

'Oh.' She groped for words; how unlike Scarlett to be helpful. 'That's kind of you, thanks.'

'Don't thank me, Channel 6's saving money

on cab fares. We're on the same route. Just be ready.'

Jade had time to shampoo and shower, but since there was nothing for breakfast in the fridge, she learned lines until she heard the buzzer.

Outside the street was deserted, grey in the early morning light. Jade's hair dripped on her shoulders as she plunged into the waiting taxi.

'Modelling for the Salvation Army?' Scarlett greeted her with raised brows.

Jade was sick of the put-downs. She scowled at Scarlett, who was shoe-horned into a dayglo red mini-skirt, a crimson chiffon shirt and red rope-soled platforms. Even her clearly visible bra was red. 'Haven't you got any other colour to wear besides red?'

Scarlett giggled. 'It's my signature. I wear my name so people won't forget me. You could wear little green Chinese fat men in your ears.'

'I'd rather be remembered for my acting.'

Laughter pealed out. 'You are such an innocent. But you're not a wimp, so I'll help you. Listen, what we do is not acting. This show is the biggest opportunity you're ever likely to get to make a name for yourself. You're a fool if you don't take it.'

'Meaning?'

'Twenty million people throughout the world see me on their screens every week night. Do you have any idea what that means?' She leaned back in the taxi seat, eyeing her suggestively.

Jade was distracted by the towering new office blocks in Macquarie Street, glittering monuments to money. It was the first time she had seen Sydney in daylight. A film of gold light flickered from the office windows.

'It means,' she continued, 'the chance to make serious money.'

'I'd rather be a great actress.' There was something repellent about the naked greed in Scarlett's eyes.

'I said take the circular road, you fool,' she yelled at the taxi driver. Fishing for her mobile in her backpack, she punched some numbers and started yelling. 'Ed? I told you never to send me new drivers. We've got an idiot here who thinks the Northern Highway will get us to Wallera.' She snapped off the phone halfway through Ed's apologies. 'What was I saying? Oh yes, money. No doubt they've got you on some miserly base rate. But don't worry about that. Go for as much exposure as possible.'

Jade had been happy with the salary her agent agreed to. After all, it was more than her step-father earned. 'I don't understand what you're talking about.'

'Fan mags. They'll pay you for interviews, specially the British ones. Then there are appearances in other people's shows. Celebrity appearances are worth a bit. Live appearances at pubs and clubs. The more you do, the more popular you become. Then you're famous just for being famous, so you get millions for doing a calendar or an ad. Who cares about acting? Look at Elle, or Madonna. They don't have to do anything any more.'

'But I love acting.' Jade was horrified.

'Wait till you've been on the 'Coast' a few weeks. Ah, here we are.' She handed the luckless driver a Cabcharge and dashed out of the cab. 'I'm due in make-up, but since we have our last scenes at two this afternoon, I'll take you shopping. You can't go round looking like a refugee.'

Dazed, Jade made her way through to the back of the studio building. The famous Scarlett Stone wanted to go shopping with her! Eat your heart out, Lee-Anne!

The back of the studios where the filming took place looked more like a second-hand warehouse than a television station. Rolls of carpet and second-hand furniture piled up to the cantilevered roof. Sound and light technicians with headphones milled around, people busied about with clip-boards. A party of school kids sat patiently at the entrance with their teacher. They ignored her.

Daniel emerged from the men's changing rooms. He was dressed as his character Jason in board shorts, his mahogany chest bare. Seeing Jade, he grinned easily and sauntered over towards her. The schoolgirls screamed. 'Enjoy the anonymity. Once you're on air you'll be public property.' One girl broke away from the group and ran towards him sobbing 'Jason' at the top of her lungs. He escaped into the studio. A security guard held the girl firmly in his arms and escorted her out to the carpark. Screams echoed faintly into the distance. 'Jason, Jason, Jason ... '

Jade knew how she felt. Sighing, she turned towards the Green Room and bumped into Scarlett.

'Gorgeous, isn't he?' Scarlett lit a cigarette. 'But don't waste your time fancying him. It's like eating peanuts.'

'Pardon?'

'Once you start, it's hard to stop. And you'll never get anywhere. He's immune to women.'

Jade didn't need to be told that, but it helped to strengthen her resolve. In the Green Room, she found Belinda reading horoscopes.

'What are you, Sagittawius?' lisped Belinda, fingering her dangling Snoopy earrings. 'You like luxury, don't you, darling?'

'Cancer, actually.'

'The crab!' She looked up from the news-paper, eager for gossip. 'I heard you attacking Scar-lett yesterday. And you got Shady Sherrilyn at lunch. Congratulations! You're going to be fun to have around.'

'Scarlett and I are friends now. We're going shopping this afternoon.' Belinda's eyes widened, but she didn't speak.

'I'm starving, where's the canteen?'

Ten minutes and a sticky bun later, Jade met up with Scarlett in make-up. Felicity was caking heavy foundation on with a sponge. Scarlett scowled into the mirror.

'My skin looks like an alien. I had a flawless complexion when I started this show.'

'Can't be helped, darl. Nothing wrong with my products, it's the lights. The heat opens your pores.' She swirled a monstrous powder brush over her cheeks. 'Finished.'

Scarlett got up and hissed in Jade's ear as she stalked out, 'They don't bloody care!'

Jade took her seat and watched mesmerised as Felicity worked the same magic as the day before. It took almost half an hour.

'Jade.' Maggie put her head round the door. 'Babe-cakes, you look divine. Don't disappear at lunchtime. *TV Times* are coming in to do a front cover. They want you and Daniel, the new "young lovers".' Maggie winked.

Jade's cheeks burned with pleasure. A front cover already! She examined the stranger in the mirror. A week ago she would have thought her appearance tarty. But she was getting used to piled-up hair and high-gloss lips. Maybe if it was part of her job . . .

'Gorgeous,' Maggie repeated firmly. 'You should think about wearing make-up all the time. You're in the public eye now, you know. You can't go around forever looking like you fell out of the back of a theatre. So boring!'

Thanking Felicity profusely and clutching her script, Jade set off for wardrobe. Behind a cur-tained-off area of the studio, she found racks of clothes labelled by the character's names. She looked for 'Kerry' and was rummaging happily through the designer-label silk and linen dresses, when she was startled by a growl.

'Don't touch. Vun mark und you're dead.' A giant crouched over an ironing board. 'Ivan, head of wardrobe,' he growled, without looking up from the frilly skirt he was spray-starching. 'Unt you are Kerry. You vare the charcoal-grey Harry Who today, with the Simona satin slip top. Lucky girl. I comming. Wait.'

Jade froze, awed by the sheer bulk of the man. You could have grated cheese on his voice, yet he handled the clothes delicately.

'Okay.' He straightened and lumbered over, looking sorrowfully at her jeans. 'You can give those poor creatures the burial they deserve and put this on.' He ushered her into a tiny booth without a mirror. Slipping on the silk and the fine Italian linen skirt, Jade began to think about the shopping trip. She had no money. Would Scarlett lend her some? How much should she spend? Maggie said she had to improve her image, part of her job. It wouldn't do to let down the show. Maybe she should buy several outfits?

The Harry Who jacket had shoulder pads and carved antique metal buttons. Even the shoes were exquisite. She emerged to face Ivan's polaroid camera.

'Amazink. Who would have believed that sub-urban child could look like this. I am a genius.'

Jade wasn't sure if it was a compliment or an

78

insult. She glanced at her watch. 'Thanks, Ivan, see you later.' She left him busily pinning up her polaroid on a huge corkboard cluttered with pictures and lists.

Her schedule told her studio two, the one she saw Daniel enter. The swing door gave way to a cavernous space lined with aluminium foil and hung with drum-sized spotlights and sheets of white polystyrene. Cameramen floated up and down on mobile cameras, attached to each other with thick cables like umbilical cords. Thicker cables snaked across the floor, coiled and looped on belts and lights. Towards the back, a tiny mock sitting-room was floodlit. Daniel stood behind the sofa, his powerful body gleaming under the spotlights, facing the actor who played Dad. It was the final take. Jade edged up to a monitor several metres away where a group of people watched the scene being filmed.

'Bags me after Scarlett.'

'Who said he was seeing Scarlett?'

'She's too cheerful this morning. Must be Dan!' They giggled quietly.

'Silence. Final take,' yelled a tall woman in overalls.

Jade stood transfixed as the camera closed in on Daniel. In the close-up she felt he was talking directly to her. His talent lay in making the audience believe they were all alone with him. And girls, Jade thought. Yesterday he made me believe he really liked me. She suppressed a stab of longing.

It was the final take. A minute or so of dialogue passed, then the director called out, 'It's a wrap.' Everyone suddenly relaxed. She guessed an hour must have passed to film the two-minute scene. Technicians and props got busy. 'Dad' rushed past her.

'That's Call-a-Cab Colin,' Belinda appeared. 'He's been on this show since it started and he can't wait to get home after his scenes. Come on, we're on now.'

There was no time to be nervous. Everyone had a job to do, and it seemed, as actors, theirs was the least important. First a quick run-through for lines. The director introduced herself and asked Jade how Kerry felt about the next scene.

'She's just arrived from Head Office, so she's nervous, but she's determined she can do a good job, if the staff of the surf shop will let her. Maybe she'll try a bit too hard, you know, want their approval.'

'Is that how you're feeling, Jade?'

'Mmm.' She hadn't seen the parallel.

'You'll do a good job.' The director grinned, then turned her attention to Belinda. After that, they blocked in movements on the small set. The slightest foot out of place or change in the angle of head could affect shooting and force another take. There were sound checks and light checks. And more rehearsals. Then more rehearsals again. Finally, on the fifteenth take, they were released. Jade staggered back to the Green Room to relax. She felt wrung out. Sweat trickled down her armpits and her face felt as though she was wearing a rubber mask. Four more scenes to go. And today was a good day.

'Wait until you have a fourteen-scene day.' Belinda poured herself a coffee. 'With an interview squeezed in.'

'Hey, Jade.' Daniel strolled in wearing a suit and tie. He was heart-meltingly attractive in full black and white evening dress. 'The photographers are here from *TV Times*.' He held out his hand and yanked her to her feet.

The shoot was taking place in the main offices at the front of Channel 6. A boardroom had been set up as a photographic studio, the back wall draped from ceiling to floor in cream muslin. Out-sized silver umbrellas faced the back and the photographer was setting up his tripod. He strode forward, arm outstretched.

'Gerald Courtney-Smythe. How do you do.' He pumped their hands briskly. 'Jade, outfits over there. Evening wear from French Connection in the UK.'

A wardrobe girl led Jade to a curtained-off area set up as a makeshift changing room. 'What do you reckon?' She held up three outfits. 'Need to re-do your face.'

Jade was resigned to it all by now. It took nearly forever to select the right face, hair and outfit. This time her eyes were toned down to allow the scarlet glossy lipstick to dominate her face. It was the exact shade of her satin slip dress. The shoe-string straps meant no bra and it was cut low all round. She felt naked.

'Isn't this a bit revealing?' She looked down, doubtfully. Her breasts were almost completely exposed. Her hair – piled up in loops and falling around her face – felt as though she'd just got out of bed.

'That's what sells magazines.' The assistant fussed with the shoes, a pair of stilettos with ruby chains for straps. She clipped dangling rubies to her ears and added a red-beaded choker. 'Anyway, I fink you look terrific.' The girl was a Londoner, over specially for the shoot. 'I did Elle last week; you look sexier. You've got better tits and bum. Lucky do'er!'

Jade was flattered. More than flattered, she was shocked. No one had ever called her sexy before.

'Listen, some faces are made for the camera. It's the bones, see. You've got even features, strong bones and good lips and teef. The right make-up can make anyone look good. But wif a good face, it's a miracle what we can do. Your face is as close to perfect as they get. People must've told you that before.'

Jade shook her head. She knew men fancied her, and Wayne once called her 'choice', but apart from that she'd always thought of herself as unusual rather than beautiful.

'You really mean that?' Maybe these people complimented the 'talent' as part of their job description. 'Is there a mirror?'

The girl led her out to a sheet of glass propped up against the window.

'It can't be me,' she gasped, staring at her reflection in wonder.

Daniel appeared. 'And they pay me for this job?' He held out his arms in mock surprise.

His expression made her laugh as she pirouetted on her six-inch heels.

A brocade antique armchair had been set up in camera. They wanted a high-class seduction shot. 'Jason' and 'Kerry', the new hot item on 'Sunshine Coast'.

'Just flirt with each other for a while, to get warmed up.' The English photographer was one of the leading *fashionistas* and used to working with international celebrities. He made them feel honoured to be allowed in his presence.

Daniel grinned and led her over to the chair. 'Did I tell you, you're the most stunning girl I've ever seen in my entire life?'

'Yes, and I don't believe you,' she grinned, shoving him away. Suddenly the ruby strap gave way and thousands of little beads clattered on the floor. Jade looked down with a gasp of horror. Silky fabric slithered down her side and completely exposed one breast.

A blinding flash of light exploded.

'Great shot!' said Courtney-Smythe. 'Marlene, the sellotape! Now keep working, this shot has to sizzle.'

Jade was almost dying of embarrassment, but

Daniel had gallantly pretended not to look. He moved straight into character as the professional seducer. He was witty, exciting and inventive as he moved around looking for new angles. He'd whisper in her ear, then kiss her neck, unclip her earrings, take off her shoe, stroke her arm, hug her towards him, or bend her over backwards like a Spanish dancer. And all the time the camera exploded, sending charges of white heat through their bodies. He was wonderful; she simply couldn't resist flowing along with the game. But it was just a game, she had to remind herself.

There was one moment when she was sitting in his lap, her legs stretched out behind them, arms around his neck. He lowered his face to hers, their lips almost touching, when she felt sure he wasn't joking. Something flickered in his eyes. She turned her face away, embarrassed.

When he spoke, his voice came out thickly. 'Look at me.'

And she did, momentarily. But the intensity frightened her.

Later, when she'd cleaned up and returned to studio to prepare for the afternoon scenes, they passed each other in the corridor. Instead of the usual joke or compliment, he smiled briefly and hurried past.

'Not like him to be sulky,' Scarlett commented. They were on their way to their first scene together, one where Scarlett's character meets Kerry and the 'jealous' storyline is set up.

'Sulky?' Jade turned to watch his retreating back. She felt uncomfortable.

'Mm,' Scarlett paused to examine her reflection in the studio mirror. 'I told him I had a date for the BAFTA Awards night. I expect he hoped I'd go with him.'

Half an hour later the director called it a 'take', congratulating them as they left. 'Well done. That scene was juicy. Jade, brilliant first debut!'

Scarlett waited until they were out of earshot then said, 'Huh! Call herself a director. She couldn't direct you to the toilets!'

Jade stepped over the power cables and out of the bright, airless studio. Perspiration ran down her sides and her throat was parched, but she'd never felt more alive. Felicity helped her clean off.

'I watched on the monitors. What a scene!'

Back in the Green Room a sign on the notice-board read 'Jade Silver, Marshall wants to see you ASAP.'

'Good luck.' Scarlett gave her a push towards the door. 'And don't forget our date this afternoon.'

She set off anxiously to the main offices. It reminded her of being sent to the headmaster at school. Marshall was in a huddle with Maggie when she went in.

'Darling!' Maggie leapt to her feet rushing forward to hug her. A row of bangles dug into her back. 'Febulous scene, simply febulous.'

'We've watched the takes from this morning, and we're delighted, Jade. Champagne?'

'No, thank you.'

'Let me pour, sweetie-pie,' Maggie seized the bottle and two outsized glasses. 'Happy, Jade?'

'Very.'

'Anything you'd like. Anything we can do for you?' Marshall accepted his glass and raised a toast.

'Well . . . ' Jade thought about Scarlett. 'I was going to go shopping this afternoon. I have no food in my flat and hardly any clothes. And no money. Would it be possible . . . ?'

'Say no more. Delighted to help out. Off you go down to Arnold, he's the accountant. I'll buzz him now, an advance of, say, a thousand dollars?'

Jade fainted at the thought of so much money. 'Thank you, both of you,' and backed out, leaving them busily topping up their glasses.

Arnold waited for her in the corridor, beckoning like a spider to a fly.

'Come in, come in, come in,' he gushed. 'Got your cash right here.'

His eyes were level with her shoulders, and she could count the single strands of hair pasted over his bald spot.

'This is so kind of you.'

'Not at all, not at all, not at all.' Grinning up at her, he let his arm slip casually round her waist. 'You're on the team, and doing very well I hear.' The hand was now resting on her bottom.

Jade made for the desk where a pile of crisp new hundred dollar bills were neatly piled. 'This mine?'

'More if you want,' he leered. 'Just sign the docket.'

She leant forward to initial the book. 'Have you always been an accountant?' she tried a conversational tone to distract him.

'I love figures,' he stared at her bottom. 'I'm good with figures,' he repeated unnecessarily.

Jade seized her money and backed out. Scarlett was waiting for her in the corridor.

'Still in one piece? He's losing his touch. Come on, David Jones will be closed soon.'

They found a taxi in the studio carpark. It smelt of cigarettes and disinfectant. Scarlett complained immediately. She grabbed the front seat, and Jade gratefully sank into the back. What a day! So much had happened. The compliments, the approval. *They love me*, she breathed, *they really love me. If only he* . . .

Through half-closed eyes, she watched the tree-lined suburbs sweep past. Spring was warming up; they passed a row of beeches bursting with new colour, daffodils thrusting out of the verges, then on towards the inner-city apartment blocks glittering in the sun.

She thought of the photographic shoot and her stomach churned. Naked in front of him! Rifling nervously through the pile of scripts on her lap, she discovered it would be a week before she had to face him on set again. Relieved, she tried to read the scene, but the effort of focusing made her carsick. Then she remembered how long it was since she'd eaten. Scarlett wasn't pleased.

'Really, Jade. Shopping is a serious business, so is eating. The two shouldn't be confused.' She sighed dramatically. 'All right, we'll grab something at DJ's.'

As they drew up in front of the vast red granite store, Scarlett leapt out, leaving Jade to hand over one of her new bills. The driver scowled and pointed to a sign which read, 'Please tender the correct fare'. Fortunately the store's doorman came to her rescue.

'Are you Miss Stone's assistant?' he asked, as soon as the taxi left.

'Apparently!'

He stood back, respectfully spinning the side entrance, injecting her into the cool expensive interior of the Parfumerie. Elegant women posed behind gold and glass counters under glittering chandeliers. They made Jade feel windblown and scruffy. There was no sign of Scarlett and her hunger pangs had grown into violent stomach spasms.

'Miss Silver?' A fearsome woman in black draped crepe approached, her voice pure Vaucluse. She whisked her up to the seventh floor where Scarlett was holding court in a private chamber. There were soft lamps glowing on the rich, dark furniture and silk Persian carpets underfoot. Scarlett drank from a porcelain tea cup and addressed the salesgirls.

'Ah, here she is now,' she smiled brilliantly at

Jade. 'Darling, I've told them all about you. All right everyone, let's go!' The room emptied.

Jade noticed a platter bearing the bones of a smoked salmon. Dirty plates were strewn over the table. Disappointed, she picked at the parsley decorations.

'That's right, tuck in. I ordered some food for you. Should be some tea left in the pot. Now for goodness sake, take off those hideous clothes.'

'I thought we were going shopping?'

'Private shopping, darling! We can't possibly wander around foraging for clothes like refugees.'

'Everyone else does.'

'Exactly. People will see us, or rather me. Then we'll have ghastly fans screaming at us. From now on, you must learn to sit back and be waited on. One of the perks.' Scarlett was finishing off her own plate of smoked salmon.

Jade glanced around at the walls of gilt-framed mirrors. Her own face came back to her, multiplied endlessly. Her hair was still dressed in the loose Claudia Schiffer way, but she'd cleaned her make-up off. Half Jade and half Kerry. *Who am I now?* she wondered.

7

Jade spent the next two hours modelling garments Scarlett chose from the armloads brought in by the sales ladies. There was a black mini-skirt and T-shirt made of the same material as her swimming costume. Heavy metal chains, hung with ruby-eyed skulls, draped around her waist and hips.

'Not short enough,' Scarlett pronounced. 'You can never wear enough make-up or have short enough skirts.'

Someone rushed forward to turn up her waistband.

'It's offensive,' Jade protested.

'Very much so,' the sales lady agreed warmly. 'All the Bondi Bodies range this year has that aggressive camp look. Very now.'

'It's a happening image,' chimed in a tiny girl with a peroxide crew cut and two eyebrow rings.

'Try it with the leather jacket,' commanded Scarlett.

Like Wayne's, she thought, slipping on a short black bomber jacket with skulls hanging from every zip. Although his wouldn't have cost over a thousand dollars.

'And the boots!'

Jade stood still while two assistants pushed her feet into high-heeled boots and laced them up to her knees.

'Wow! You won't be safe in public.'

'Amazing with the hair!'

'Fabulous.' 'Stunning.' 'Fantastic.'

Jade was sedated by perfumes, soft insinuating compliments, angelic music, rich fabrics and colours. By the time she was ushered out into the harsh reality of Elizabeth Street she was fainting with a surfeit of luxury. In contrast, the street outside looked like a war zone, dizzying daylight, roaring traffic and the unbearable stench of petrol. Confused and unsteady in thigh-high black lace-up boots, she stumbled into a magazine stand, dropping one of her black and white chequered bags. It was the one holding her Versace silver wet-look evening dress. It slithered out of the black tissue like a live snapper and lay amongst a scattering of *TV Times*. Images of Scarlett's wet red grin decorated the pavement, making a pattern on the rough grey surface.

Where was Scarlett? Then she remembered Scarlett rushing off halfway through the clothes-buying session, taking their shared Cabcharge by mistake. How much money had she spent? The notes Sam had given her were mostly still in her pocket. Oh, yes! Someone had helpfully opened a DJ's account. Nothing had been too much trouble. She glanced down at her tight skirt and boots. Her old clothes had been discreetly removed. Well, she had Scarlett to thank for all this; her advice had been invaluable. Straightening up, she hailed a taxi. 'Paradise Towers,' she commanded, imitating Scarlett, and collapsed exhausted into the back.

'Been doing some spending, ma'am?' Ben the doorman greeted her, taking the packages as he ushered her into the lift.

'Got to look the part.'

'My wife loves shopping, only we can't afford too much of it.' He flashed strong even teeth.

Jade reached in her pocket for a tip. 'A present for her, then.' She handed over a hundred dollar bill. It felt good to hear him laugh with pleasure.

Letting herself into her beautiful apartment felt wonderful. *All mine*, she gloated, throwing down her bags, admiring the spectacular view. After she'd hung up the Versace, two casual Val Morgan outfits and a Donna Karan dress, the only one she had chosen herself, she set about making dinner. There was a tiny red eye winking on her answering machine, but she decided it could wait. What couldn't wait was unloading the delicious things she'd picked up in DJ's Food Hall. That had been the best part of the afternoon.

The ladies had helpfully taken her down there

when she'd told them about her empty fridge. And it was bliss. She'd wandered entranced past giant tiger prawns heaped on mountains of ice, armies of pink lobsters, loaves of bread as long as your arm, sweet-smelling pastries and strange bottles and jars from faraway places like Zanzibar and Reykjavik. Nothing like the Borringup Hypermart. *I'll always shop here*, she thought, piling up her trolley.

Her fridge now looked magical filled with smoked salmon, fresh gnocchi, hazelnut yoghurt, frozen profiteroles and a selection of beautiful-looking vegetables. After that she suddenly felt too weak to actually do any cooking, so she munched on some profiteroles while learning her lines for the next day. By ten, she had collapsed on her queen-sized bed, exhausted.

The next day and the day after that, the pattern was set. Her alarm would ring at five, too early to eat, barely time to shampoo and squeeze herself into one of her Val Morgan outfits before the taxi driver summoned her on the intercom. Most days Scarlett would be in the taxi first, complaining bitterly about something. At first this irritated Jade, then she grew used to it, and finally she found herself joining in.

'I know what you mean,' she agreed, listening to Scarlett's latest outraged tirade against Marshall. Or 'Me too,' when she moaned about the damage make-up was doing to her skin. There was only one subject she kept silent about. Daniel Hunter. Scarlett had many theories to explain why he wasn't in love with her. He was anally repressive, or a misogynist. 'What's a misogynist?' Jade asked. 'A poofter,' Scarlett confided.

But she knew better. They'd had several scenes together by the end of her second week on the show. On set their eyes tangled as he stood, brooding and aloof. She would find herself stuttering and dropping scripts, waiting for the call 'Action'. Then they would be face to face, acting out the early stages of a romance. It was nerve-racking. Sweat poured down her sides as her confidence drained away.

In one scene he stood behind her, as Jason, and touched her shoulder. 'Kerry, I think you know what I've come for.' As she turned to face the full intensity of his eyes, a muscle moved in his cheek. She thought she would black out from the pain of her heart crashing around like jeans in a spin-drier. 'No, tell me,' she had to answer, the directions said 'arrogantly'. And he drew his finger slowly down her cheek and across her lips without speaking. Then she had to slap his face and say, 'Never touch me again.' Everything went wrong that day, and the scene was shot over twenty times before the final cut. Afterwards, she ran to make-up panic-stricken to check her face. How could she look so cool and perfect when her insides were churning?

Belinda noticed what was going on. 'You've got a cwush on him,' she charged, eating chocolates from a pink satin box a fan had sent.

'No. Well, a bit. It's an old schoolgirl thing. I'll get over it.'

'I didn't,' smiled Belinda kindly, holding out the box.

But she wasn't so sure. If it wasn't for Daniel Hunter, her life would be sheer bliss. He'd changed since the first day. Now, he avoided her, leaving the Green Room the minute she walked in. What happened to 'Call me if you need a friend'?

Everyone else was fabulous. They waited on her, listened to her opinions, complimented and thanked her. They said she was wonderful and talented and gorgeous and intelligent.

And Scarlett had been the best. Who was it who showed her the fashionable sushi restaurants, and taught her to sound bored as she ordered her coffee, 'A double de-caff capp, thanks'? And helped her buy the latest digital mobile? And took her clubbing at the weekend? Without Scarlett, she'd still be a dull suburban girl with no style.

It was a Wednesday evening, several weeks after she joined the show, when Daniel made his first contact. Jade was at home in the kitchen trying to slice beans. The phone rang, piercing the silence. Startled, she cut her finger and blood fell in bright spots as she ran for the phone.

'Hi, it's Dan.'

Jade's heart stopped.

'May I come round and talk to you?'

'Yes.' Jade sucked her finger, hoping she didn't sound too eager.

'Now?'

'Sure,' she mumbled, her mouth full of finger.

The phone clicked off. Sprinting, she showered, painted her face and pulled herself into a wet-look tank top with silver leather jeans. She was about to switch on the stereo when the doorbell rang.

Despite her high silver shoes, he was still several inches taller than her. His face looked sombre, the eyes dark and watchful. Heroine stood behind him, wagging her tail.

'I need to talk to you.'

She led them into her sitting room overlooking the city, which glittered like diamonds against black velvet.

'It's about Scar ... ' he began, but the phone rang and Jade was forced to answer it.

'Hello, Jade. I've been trying to call you, but there was only your answering machine. Did you get my messages?' Margaret Silver sounded distressed.

'I can't talk now. I'll call you back.' Jade put the receiver down firmly. Smiling brightly, she called out, 'Would you like some tea, or coffee, or champagne?' Scarlett said you must always keep champagne on ice, in case.

'Tea for me. Any ginger snaps for Heroine?'

There weren't. All she had left were the beans and an aubergine whose glorious deep purple glossy skin was now wrinkled and dull.

Setting down the teapot and cups she apologised for the lack of biscuits. 'I never seem to have time to go shopping.'

'At least you keep up with the housework.'

'That's my mother's influence.'

'How much influence does she have with you?' He looked her directly in the eye.

Jade wondered what he was getting at. 'Same as any mother. What influence does your mother have on you?'

'I haven't got a mother.' He ignored her crestfallen expression. 'I'm here because I know how hard it is to survive on your own, especially in a city like Sydney. And you seem to have no support. Maggie says you auditioned and signed contracts without any family with you.'

'I didn't want them with me. I've always managed my affairs by myself.' Heroine had come out from behind his legs and was licking her hand, chocolatey eyes full of sadness and affection.

'Sometimes there are risks in being too alone.'

Jade felt her heart leap. Maybe this was his roundabout way of asking for a date.

'Like what?' she prompted. Then hopefully, 'You've come here to say something. What is it?'

He stood up and paced the thick white carpet. He looked dark and brooding against the pale blue and antique white furnishings. The room vibrated with his masculine presence. 'You see a lot of Scarlett, don't you?'

Jade assented.

'You two have some things in common. Talent, guts,' he paused, eyes twinkling, 'looks. But she's very different to you. She can be heartless.'

Jade was stung. 'How can you accuse her of

heartlessness? She's done so much for me. More than anyone else on the show.' She looked at him pointedly, shocked to hear a tremor in her voice.

Daniel glanced away quickly. 'I'm sorry I haven't been able to talk to you much; I've been terribly busy. Look, the thing is, when someone goes all out to be friendly, you have to ask why. Marshall once gave me great advice. He said, 'Always hold the question *why are they telling me this?* in your mind.'

Jade looked at him steadily, then said, 'Why are you telling me this?'

'Because I care what happens to you.'

Jade could hear the kitchen clock ticking, loud in the silence. *Oh, why doesn't he ask me for a date, move over to join me on the sofa, find out my star sign? Anything?* But he sat still, stroking Heroine, long fingers curling and threading through her creamy fur.

'Are you telling me I shouldn't be friends with her?'

'It's not my place to tell you what to do.' He looked at his watch.

He really doesn't care at all, she thought, swallowing back a lump in her throat. 'So why did you come here tonight?'

He gazed at her steadily for a moment, looking strangely vulnerable.

The phone rang again. While she was answering it, she heard the soft click of her front door. Choking back her tears, she shouted into the receiver,

'What!'

'It's Mum. Jade, I have to talk to you.'

'I can't talk now, my heart is broken. Tomorrow.' She slammed down the phone, found her gold compact, clutched it to her heart and lay face down on the gold satin bedspread.

And that was how she found herself when a ringing phone woke her the next morning. Her alarm clock said eight o'clock. For a moment she thought she'd missed a taxi call, but then remembered her first scene wasn't until ten.

'Jade, it's Mum. Can you come down next weekend? It's urgent.'

'I can't just pop down to Borringup, it'll take hours,' she moaned, stretching her legs, stiff from sleeping in jeans.

'Your Grandpa is seriously ill. He might not make it this time. Please, Jade, it could be the last time you'll see him.'

Jade thought of the cast party on Friday. Of her quarrel with Daniel. Of the chance to lie around on Saturday morning and recover from the stress of sixteen-hour days. Of cappuccinos and gossip with Scarlett in their favourite new cafe in Quayside.

'Do I have to?' The silence on the other end was pathetic. 'Okay, but I won't be able to get there until Saturday afternoon. And I'll have to leave on Sunday morning.'

'We'll pick you up. Call me with your flight times.'

'*He* will complain; just get Wayne to pick me up.'

The rest of the week was frantic. She had too many scenes and hardly time to think, let alone cook at night. The only time she saw Daniel, he was on set and didn't seem to notice her. Their next love scene was a big one, but not scheduled until the following week. By that time her character would finally hit the screens and her life would change forever.

It already has changed, she thought. It was Saturday afternoon when she tramped down the gangway of the Qantas flight to Melbourne. It seemed like a lifetime ago since she walked up this same gangway to start her new life. I'm not the same girl who left Borringup, she thought as she caught sight of her reflection in a plate-glass window. And it's not only because of the Sydney clothes.

Her parents were there to meet her, looking smaller and greyer. All three stood around like strangers, unsure how to react.

'Where's Wayne?' she asked.

'Didn't he talk to you?' Her mother looked nervously at her step-father.

'Good flight?' he asked, changing the subject.

They made their way out to the old Volvo.

'Darling,' her mother began, 'isn't that skirt a little short?'

'It's the fashion, Mum.'

'But I thought you didn't like too much make-up or . . .'

'Don't be ridiculous. I can hardly go around looking like a dreeb.' Without noticing, she drawled like Scarlett.

The drive home was the most depressing journey she'd ever made. Her mother droned on about Grandpa, it started to drizzle and her stepfather let off wind more than once.

They drove straight to the hospital so that Jade could see her grandfather. They found him propped upright like a rag doll on a pile of starched white pillows. Her mother drew the curtains around the bed and pulled up a chair for Jade to sit in, as if she were the honoured guest. Clear plastic tubes festooned his body. One came out of his nose, another from his wrist and one from under the bedclothes. It was attached to a plastic bladder filled with urine on the vinyl floor. Jade almost gagged. Struggling to keep a sympathetic smile on her face, she reached out to take his hand. It lay dry and cool in her palm, like an autumn leaf. His eyes, redrimmed and faded, stared vacantly up at the ceiling.

'Does he know we're here?' she whispered to her mother.

'Sometimes. Keep talking to him, let him know who you are.'

Jade swallowed hard. 'Grandpa,' she began, searching her memories for something that might connect. 'It's Jade, your White Angel, remember?' When she was little and the only child, she and her mother had lived with Grandpa, before Grandma died. There had been a dressing-up box in their house, with a white sheet and a wire halo. It had been Jade's favourite angel outfit. His eyelids flickered, then slowly he looked towards her, focusing on her face.

'Angel . . . ' His voice was just a breath of air.

Jade's heart constricted. She remembered him tall and strong, throwing her up into the sky, pressing fifty-cent pieces into her hand, feeding her Violet Crumbles when her mother wasn't watching. He had really loved her, before Alzheimer's destroyed his mind. And she'd forgotten his love, finding every excuse possible to avoid visiting him. Tears welled up in her eyes. She leant forward and kissed his cold forehead.

He was staring at the ceiling again when they left. Jade had to listen to her mother burbling on about what a miracle it was that he remembered her, and how this might be the turning point. Jade resisted the impulse to tell her mother to face facts. Reality had never been her strong point.

As they drove into the familiar streets of Borringup, past the playgrounds and schools she grew up in, and finally into the little street of red brick federation houses, she felt both trapped and frightened.

'Here we are!' her mother turned round to smile brightly as they drew up by the picket fence. Samantha was waiting in the front garden.

'You look like a slut,' she yelled the minute she saw Jade. The twins had been eating chocolate and struggled to be picked up, making handprints on her white lycra skirt. The house seemed smaller and shabbier than she remembered. Her mother suddenly had more important things to do and went upstairs. Apart from Samantha, who pestered her with stupid questions about 'Sunshine Coast', no one seemed interested in her. Then Wayne appeared. The room fell silent.

'What are you doing here?'

'I was babysitting, with ... ' Lee-Anne edged in behind him, gripping his hand and holding one of the twins with the other.

'What is *she* doing here?' Jade's voice rose.

'I tried to tell you, but there was only an answering machine.' He looked sheepish.

'You pasty-faced conniving slag! How long has this been going on?' Jade glared at Lee-Anne.

'What's Belinda like?' Samantha plucked at Jade's skirt.

'Clear off, and take my bag to my room,' Jade commanded.

'It's my room now. Mum put a mattress down on the twins' floor for you.' Samantha had the grace to look apologetic.

Jade was furious. Displaced, forgotten, tossed out on the scrapheap! She was preparing to destroy Lee-Anne when her step-father walked in.

'Now you're back, you'll be able to give your Mum a hand with the laundry. She's had no time to do anything this week, running back and forwards to the hospital.'

'What's wrong with your legs?' Jade

exploded. This was the last straw. How dare he assume she'd buckle down and skivvy. 'I work a sixty-hour week, you know. I need a break at the weekends, which I've given up to visit Grandpa.'

His eyes bulged out of his head, but her mother came back before he had a chance to draw breath.

'Well, if it was that much trouble, I wouldn't have asked you.' She switched on both taps at once, so Jade had to shout.

'Why the hell am I on the floor in their room?' she yelled at her mother's back. 'You know it smells of dead dogs.'

'Don't you dare barge in here yelling at everybody like Lady Muck. It's not your home any more!' Her step-father cranked up, predictable as ever.

Wayne smirked.

It was Lee-Anne who tried to calm everything down. 'Jade, I'm really sorry about that time at Giorgio's. I sent you flowers to apologise when I heard you really had met Daniel Hunter.'

Jade remembered the delphiniums. She'd hoped they were from Daniel. *Oh, God. Why is home such a nightmare?* She didn't really mind so much about losing Wayne, but to Lee-Anne? The taps turned off and the sound of her mother's sobbing took over.

'Now look what you've done. Home five minutes and you've upset everyone. Since you left, there's been no trouble. And now it's chaos again!

You ... ' He glared at Jade, taking a step forward. Sensing trouble, her mother grabbed the twins and ushered them upstairs. Samantha followed.

Wayne and Lee-Anne backed out muttering excuses. Jade saw them to the front door. He said, 'Sorry, Jade. About, you know ... '

'It's okay. I understand.'

But his parting shot ruined it. 'Don't they feed you at Channel 6? You're as thin as a dipstick. I can count your ribs.'

'You can't count, you cretinous weasel.' She slammed the door on both of them. Her face in the hall mirror looked drawn. Haggard would be more honest. Left alone in the kitchen, she hunted around for something to eat. But dinner had been cleared away and the biscuit barrel was empty. Welcome home, Jade! The sound of a lullaby drifted down the stairs. Mum was singing the twins to sleep. She remembered lying awake at night, listening to her singing to Samantha. Did she ever sing for me? Jade couldn't remember. A tiny rough tongue scratched across her leg. Marlon came out from his hiding place under the table.

She scooped him up, buried her face in his fur and wept like a baby.

8

The visit to Borringup was a complete disaster. Everything possible went wrong, including an air traffic strike which delayed her return to Sydney. The only bright spark was that her grandpa had rallied a bit. At least her mother was more cheerful now. But leaving her this time was easy. No regrets. Let them all stew, she thought, as she picked up her suitcase and strode out across the royal-blue carpet towards the taxi rank.

It was midnight, a bad time to be alone in Sydney. To her right, in the darkness, she made out a newsstand, locked up for the night. A new *TV Times* poster sealed in a wire grid bore the headline, 'A Sizzling New Star'. She hardly recognised the stunning blonde, lips turned up to be kissed. Daniel's face dominated the picture, bending down to hers in the classic romantic pose. It was the shot when he'd commanded her to look at him. Her heart stopped. The expression in his eyes! It was unmistakably desire. Could he just have been acting? Transfixed, she didn't notice a shadowy figure looming out of the toilet block by the petrol pumps.

'Give us your bag, quick!' the voice rasped.

Jade jumped back, startled to see a boy her own age in torn jeans and checked shirt, an ugly mouth and slitted, frightened eyes. A nauseating smell of stale nicotine and alcohol poisoned the night.

'Don't be silly, I've only got credit cards and you'll go to prison for using them.' Her legs turned to jelly. They were eye to eye now, and he was trembling. He flicked his eyes to the right, settling on her image on the magazine. In the distance she heard a dustbin rolling over, powered by the wind. The next second he went berserk, screeching obscenities, calling her a rich bitch and clawing at her bag. She fought back instinctively, breathing his fetid breath, numb to the pain. She didn't see the taxi driver leap out and throw himself between them.

'You should have let me go after him,' he said finally, as Jade limped towards the car.

'He was just a kid.' She couldn't stop shivering.

'You put up quite a fight!' He slipped behind the wheel, switching on the radio.

Jade huddled beside him. A fighter! Everyone thinks I'm so strong. If only they knew how terrified I really am most of the time. As for 'A Sizzling

New Star'! I can't even keep Wayne interested, and Daniel either hates me or thinks I'm stupid, or both. I must be the only virgin in the whole TV industry.

Paradise Towers had never been more welcome. The moment she reached her room, she ripped off her clothes, turned the stereo to maximum and filled the jacuzzi. But all the soap bubbles in the world couldn't wash away the smell of that poor, mad street kid. Scraping at her skin she remembered the *TV Times* image. *I want Daniel*, she thought. *I've never wanted anyone so badly. I don't even care if I lose my job. I could die tomorrow at the hands of a crazed fan, like John Lennon, and I'd never have known what it was like to be loved by Daniel Hunter. Or by anyone*, she thought bleakly, remembering the awful weekend at home. Otis Redding sang 'When a man loves a woman'. Jade closed her eyes and sang along, bitter tears rolling down her cheeks.

The next morning she bounced back, the mugger forgotten. Her immaculate kitchen gleamed in the spring sunshine. *I'm a fighter*, she thought, foraging around for breakfast. Unfortunately, there was still nothing but the aubergine, which had grown penicillin over the weekend. Grabbing a bar of chocolate, she bounded out to the waiting taxi, wet hair dripping down her neck. Scarlett was pleased to see her.

'How do you make a guy like you?' Jade demanded as soon as the door crashed shut.

'Meaning who?' Scarlett snapped off half the chocolate and dropped it into a perfectly scarlet mouth.

Instinctively, Jade said, 'Oh, you know, in general.'

'You treat them badly, for one.' Scarlett sat back and launched into her favourite subject. 'Totally ignore them. No, scrub that. Abuse them openly. Humiliate them, preferably in public.'

'But you treat everyone like that.'

'That's why they love me. Why do you think I'm the star of the show, not you or Belinda?'

Jade was stumped.

'Because I don't give a toss. Your problem is you're too nice. I heard you thanking Felicity last week for touching you up mid-take. Why do you think she's paid?'

Jade rolled down the window. Sometimes Klein's Obsession was hard to take on an empty stomach.

She thought about the advice later. Daniel was in make-up talking to Felicity. He paused as she came in, then said, 'Sorry I left so quickly last week'. Then he hesitated.

He's thinking up some excuse, Jade thought furiously, unscrewing a bottle of moisturising cream. 'No problem. I was waiting for a call.'

'Oh.' Felicity perked up. 'Someone nice?'

'Heavenly. Slim, blond and not an actor,' Jade confided. She was gratified to see him look annoyed. 'By the way, Daniel, the *TV Times* is out.

You look like Errol Flynn on speed.'

'And you sound like Scarlett!' He stormed out.

That night, Jade appeared on the screen for the first time. She celebrated by remembering to buy a frozen dinner for one, and another packet of profiteroles for dessert. She still appreciated the silence of her flat, the freedom to dance alone, the absence of children, and having her own bathroom. But it would have been nice to share it with someone.

Nestling down into the cream satin sofa, a tray of steaming tandoori chicken on her lap and a glorious plate of sticky profiteroles de-freezing on the floor, she flicked the remote control. Crashing waves and wild yells mingled with the titles music. She gave it maximum volume. Seconds later her image filled the screen. They'd filmed her strolling on a beach in a tiny pale-blue bikini, staring moodily out to sea, hair streaming out behind like a silver banner. Full body make-up gave her skin a warm glow. *Jade Silver as Kerry*, ran the titles. *I hope Wayne and Lee-Anne are watching*, she gloated. Then Daniel's titles came up. He grinned easily into the camera, body glistening with water as he heaved himself out of the sea. *Oh, God, if only he wasn't so beautiful!*

Their first love scene was scheduled to take place the next day on location at Sandy Bay on the North Shore. Jade woke feeling sick with nerves. Pick-up was at five o'clock, so there was no time to read her script again. It would take an hour to reach the shooting location. A whole hour to work

110

up a sweat. She was frankly terrified. It was one thing to act cool around him, another to stay cool while he was kissing her.

She drew up in her taxi in the Sandy Bay car park just after sunrise. Over on the sand she could see a huddle of technicians under a red and white striped umbrella. A cramped caravan used for make-up was parked beside the pantechnicons carrying sound and film equipment. Jade wandered in, half expecting Daniel to be there. It was empty. Then Felicity clattered up the steps eating a crois-sant and talking into a screechy mobile phone to the director on the beach. Through the tiny window she could make out Daniel in the distance, enjoying the surf on a Malibu board. The broad surface allowed him to stand straight and take the wave right into shore.

'What a body,' Felicity grinned, joining her. 'Poor me! I'll just have to touch him up again when he gets out of the water.'

'Full body?' Jade hated having every inch of her skin made-up.

'Fraid so, darl. Strip.'

They were almost finished when the intercom crackled. 'Okay,' Felicity nodded, 'she'll be down in a minute.' She turned to Jade. 'You're wanted, and tell Dan to get his ass up here. Tell him I'm ready, willing and able!'

Jade made her way down to the beach clutch-ing her script and an umbrella. Even the morning sun could damage her skin. Other girls wore robes between takes, but that would smudge her body make-up. Her hair had been dried loose and soft.

Kerry is sunbathing, she read from her script, *eyes closed, luxuriating in the warmth. Jason emerges from the sea. He stands before her, blotting out the sun. A sprinkle of cold water startles her awake. 'Are you waiting for anyone?' he says. Kerry's expression tells him what he wants to know. Dropping on to his knees, he takes her in his arms and kisses her gently. Kerry opens her eyes. Jason touches a finger to her eyes and says, 'You've been crying,' then holds her. Cut to . . .*

'We'll try not to muff this with a lot of takes. Marshall wants the scene to be emotional.' It was a new director; Jade hadn't worked with him before. He led her to the spot. Props had placed a brightly coloured beach towel under the swing arm of the outdoor sound mike, looking like a fluffy poodle on a stick. 'Lie here and we'll run the checks.'

Jade lay back and closed her eyes. She felt Felicity dust her face with powder, heard the cameramen's voices on the intercom. Ivan adjusted her bikini top carefully, so as not to embarrass her. Someone brushed her hair into a fan around her head. More gloss was stroked onto her lips.

'Are the chicks happy with the checks?' It was the director. Everyone laughed, then the clapperboard and 'Scene two, take one'.

Everything went still. In the silence, Jade heard the soft splash of Daniel emerging from the sea. Pale morning sun warmed her stomach and legs. She began to feel giddy. Sand crunched underfoot, drawing closer. Then everything went dark. Startled, she rose on to her elbows to see his face, inches from hers, shadowed and dangerous. She felt the feather touch of his breath on her cheek, smelt the ocean. Tilting her face imperceptibly, she gave herself up to the moment, reassured by the experienced way he cupped her head in his hands, his thumbs resting lightly on her throat. Then the lightest of brushes as his lips grazed hers.

'Cut!'

Daniel leapt to his feet, avoiding her eyes.

'Sorry, we have noise interference. Back to first position, Daniel.'

Jade's heart was wildly out of control. Gratefully, she sank back on the towel. Actors were not supposed to feel anything when they kissed in camera. Why was her body reacting like this?

Once more she had to endure the waiting. Then the sudden shock of cold sea water, her cue to sit up. This time she tried to read his expression. But his face was shadowed against the sun. She felt his arm, strong against her back as he drew her upwards towards him, then his lips on hers, softly at first, becoming slowly more insistent. Her body began to tremble, flooding with warmth, aching for more. Yet she made no move, passively allowing the kiss, as if in a dream. Then gradually, she sensed his withdrawal. Her skin tingled as he tenderly traced her features.

'You've been crying,' he whispered.

Jade flickered her eyelashes, fearfully. He was looking deep into her eyes, fingertips stroking back the curtain of hair. It was like drowning.

'Cut! We'll let it go like that. Bloody good take!'

The spell was broken. Shaking, Jade scrambled to her feet and made off for the caravan, embarrassed and flustered and triumphant, all at the same time. Showering, she listened to Felicity chatting.

'It's my friend,' she was saying. 'She's going out with this heavy-duty, big-time married man. And it's like, grab a life. I mean he's never going to leave his wife. She comes running whenever he whistles. What a loser!'

'Scarlett said men were only interested in you if you ignored them?' Jade took off the bikini and started dressing.

'Men are only interested in you when you want them, and show it. Know what I mean? They like a safe bet. By the way, how is yours, the one you were waiting for the night Dan dropped in?'

'I haven't shown him I want him yet.'

'Does he like you?' Felicity was rinsing out her sponges, and squinting out to sea where Daniel crashed into shore on a breaker.

'I'm not sure. When he kissed me it felt as though he did, but at other times he completely ignores me.'

'Who is he, anyone I know?'

Jade grabbed her bag and made for the door. 'Probably not, bye.' Her taxi back to the studio was waiting and she had seven more scenes to do that day.

Later, in the Green Room, she found a message from Marshall. He was looking healthier than usual when she ran him down in the canteen eating salad, grinning from ear to ear.

'Congratulations. I've seen this morning's take, and the reaction to your front cover in the *Times* is one of the best first day's sales they've ever had. And the ratings are up, up, up!'

Her exhaustion disappeared immediately.

'I want you to go to Melbourne at the weekend. The big Motor Show is on. I had Scarlett down to open it with Dan, but I'm sending you instead. Let's fan the public interest now we've got it. Want a celery stick?'

'No thanks. And thank you so much, I'd love to go.' She turned to leave, then asked, 'What was it you wanted to warn me about when I first arrived?'

Marshall's brow furrowed, then cleared. 'Doesn't matter any more. Have a good time,' and he waved her away, slurping a mug of fennel tea.

Belinda was concerned when she heard about the trip next day. 'A bit wisky, darling. I mean, first of all Scarlett won't be too pleased. Then you'll be alone with Daniel. You know he's never sewious about girls and with your cwush, you could be in twubble.'

Jade turned to make herself a cup of coffee when the Green Room door flew open, pinning Jade against the wall.

'Where is the traitorous slag!' Scarlett fumed.

'I suppose you mean me.' Jade fell out from behind the door, rubbing her nose.

'Serves you right, you ingratiating, snivelling, sneak. That was my trip! I had a new outfit bought and a date with Alevin Starr organised in Melbourne. Now I'll have to pay my own fare.'

'Alevin Starr!' squeaked Belinda, 'How do you know him?'

'I know everybody, and you,' she glowered a warning at Jade, 'better not forget it!' She flounced out.

Jade's nose had recovered the next morning as she waited in the Golden Gate private lounge at Sydney Airport, packed, dressed and ready for her first big promotional gig as Kerry. She was wearing the simple grey Donna Karan linen dress. Her hair was loose, and she wore just enough make-up to emphasise her eyes. A few business men glanced over at her as they rustled their papers. The smell of coffee, seafood, after-shave and cigar smoke perfumed the room. Jade was getting used to luxury. Why not, she thought, nestling into the maroon velvet cushions and accepting a lobster crudite from a passing flunkey. I'm a celebrity now.

'Darling, sorry we're late. Dan and I shared a taxi.' Scarlett had regained her composure and was sailing across the gold embossed carpet towards

116

her, dragging Daniel by the hand. Her skin-tight crimson dress barely covered her bottom and she'd pulled her auburn curls on top of her head with several yards of red chiffon. An Indian businessman nearby choked into his coffee. Kissing the air on either side of Jade's head, she stroked her nose apologetically.

'No damage.' Jade smiled, relieved the quarrel was over. Daniel was studying his schedule awkwardly. Their eyes had caught for a moment, then he'd given her a brotherly grin. It was their first meeting since the beach scene. He wore a denim shirt with rolled up sleeves and jeans and every other man in the room suddenly looked old and dull.

'I see we're booked into the Regent, which is where they're holding the big dinner after the show. Ivan told me he's sent over full evening gear.' He sat next to her; Scarlett flopped down on the other side.

Jade stared fixedly at the black hairs on his forearms and fought an irresistible desire to stroke them. He smelt of lemons. 'Where are you staying, Scarlett?'

'Probably with Alevin's group. They're playing at the Entertainment Centre. I was going to offer to get you tickets, but since you're on duty tonight, I won't tempt you.'

Jade couldn't contain her curiosity. 'Where on earth did you meet Alevin? The Frothing Alsatians are the biggest rock group in the world. My mother

117

used to go to their concerts when she was a hippie.'

'When you're hot,' she wriggled, brushing something invisible from her chest, 'every door opens. Don't expect to see me on Monday.'

'He's old enough to be your father,' Daniel snorted.

'He's rich enough to buy me diamonds, which is more to the point.' Scarlett chipped petulantly at her nail polish. 'And I've heard he's fed up with that seven-foot dragon woman he married, so I'm in with a chance of the billionaire list yet.'

The flight to Melbourne was excruciating. Daniel sat so near, their arms brushed continually. When he spoke, his mouth was inches from hers, yet he continued to treat her like a sister.

They were met at the airport by a finger-snapping, aggressive yuppie who introduced himself as 'your motor man for today, call me Wheels.' Scarlett knew an easy mark when she saw one and asked him sweetly to arrange her transport. That kept him busy, and by the time he came back a small crowd had gathered. A teenage girl about the same age as Jade asked her if she was 'hooking in to Jason', and why did she fight with Scarlett's character?

'It's just a show,' Jade tried explaining. 'We're actors, it's not real,' she went on, seeing the blank incomprehension in her eyes. Wheels suddenly remembered what he was there for.

'Back off, everyone, come on, give the stars some space!'

He clapped his hands, and the crowds parted like the Red Sea. He led Daniel and Jade out to the street where a sleek yellow Cadillac and a chauffeur waited. Daniel helped Jade in courteously, as if she were a stranger, tucking in the hem of her dress. Wheels leaped in beside her in the back, plying her with questions about her private life. Stifling a yawn, she gazed out of the tinted window as they shot off through the dingy outer suburbs of Melbourne. She saw a group of kids huddled outside McDonalds sharing a cigarette; in the window of a coffee shop a young couple kissed over the table; a family crossing the park threw sticks for a black spaniel. From the luxury of the Cadillac the world looked as unreal as a TV screen. Passing Carlton Street, she remembered a Saturday afternoon when she'd been a hopeful nobody, like millions of others. Suddenly she felt sad, as if she'd lost something.

'Time for a quick shower, luvvies, then I'll beam you over to the show. The crowds are cosmic.' He flashed a wall of teeth, then punched at his mobile again.

The Regent turned out to be a miracle of glass, gold and marble. Daniel insisted on carrying her bags and the Chinese concierge, recognising him, ran to summon the lift, bowing so low his fringe brushed the carpet.

'We're on the same floor,' he smiled impersonally, even though they were alone. 'I'll meet you downstairs.'

119

Her room was as rich and opulent as a French palace, and not long ago Jade would have danced for joy. But she ground her teeth in frustration. *Why is he treating me like a sister?* she thought furiously. *Well, if he won't respond to me, let's see what Kerry can do.*

The bathroom was even more sumptuous than her own at the Towers, but she barely noticed that either. Unzipping her oyster satin toiletries bag, she threw a whole container of Beautiful bath gels into the black marble spa, then wrenched on the gold taps. Her 'Kerry' dress and an evening dress were hanging neatly in the wardrobe; Ivan had organised everything perfectly. Shoes, stockings, accessories, and an exquisite basket of roses with 'Show 'em, darl' signed by Felicity and Ivan. Jade felt momentarily humbled. She knew how little they earned and how much the flowers must have cost.

Ripping off her clothes, she plunged into the perfumed water, letting the scented foam caress her skin. *This is my big chance*, she thought, ducking under to soak her hair. After a few blissful minutes, she dried herself carefully, massaging orchid oil over every inch of her body. Her teeth had to be brushed and flossed, rinsed and gargled. A special gloss treatment from Felicity gave her hair extra lustre.

Then her face. By now Jade was a master of the art. Stepping back, she admired her reflection. The tight crocus-yellow, scooped-neck dress was borderline Kerry, almost too sexy. Ivan is determined to have me outshine Scarlett, she thought, wobbling on one leg as she clipped on her Italian stilettos.

The hotel phone rang. 'Luvvie, we're a teensie bit late!' Wheels sounded frantic.

'On my way.' She sprayed more Beautiful and whisked off down to the lift.

As she emerged into the foyer, Wheels' jaw dropped. 'Wow!'

Daniel stood up. 'You'd have been better off in flat shoes; it's going to be a long day,' he said, and held open the door for her.

'I'm appearing as Kerry,' she snapped, hopping to catch up with him. After all that effort!

He was the same at the stadium. Wheels ushered them into a back room behind the main stage. The theme music from 'Sunshine Coast' blasted through the auditorium, whipping up excitement and gathering the crowds. Jade could feel the sweat trickling down her armpits. Her first public appearance.

'Do I look all right?' she asked Daniel, peering over his shoulder at the sea of faces. In the distance, glittering metallic cars revolved on raised platforms, their doors and bonnets open like monster flying-beetles preparing to take off.

'You're fine,' he murmured absently, not even looking round. 'Let's go!' Grabbing her hand, he charged into the centre of the spots as a huge roar went up.

Blinded by light, Jade felt the energy lift her

up. Daniel took the microphone and introduced himself. A heckler yelled, 'Where's Scarlett?'

'She couldn't make it, but every cloud has a silver lining. Please welcome the latest star of "Sunshine Coast", Jade Silver.'

Another roar went up and Jade thrilled to the sound. The excitement was intoxicating. Flashlights exploded on all sides. He kept a tight hold on her hand throughout, taking questions from the audience about their on-screen romance, answering gallantly, pulling her towards him occasionally to kiss the side of her head to the delight of the crowds. Later, when they set up tables for autograph signing, Jade found herself face to face with the blanket adoration she'd seen fans give Daniel. As if she were different, something greater than a human being.

After the signings, they were whisked away to meet promoters and sponsors; then there were hours of photographic shoots with various car manufacturers. By late afternoon, Jade was exhausted. Daniel remained unfailingly polite and as remote as an iceberg. She wanted to scream.

'Look this way, Miss Silver,' called yet another photographer, 'and Mr Hunter, could you put your arm around her shoulders? Lovely.'

Jade clicked on her professional smile, licked her lips, hitched up her skirt a fraction, then froze. There, on the other side of the barrier rope, were Wayne, Lee-Anne and Samantha, like a perfect little family, waving and cheering.

9

'What the hell are you doing here?' Jade demanded, as soon as Wheels settled them all in a small office behind the Ford stand. He'd persuaded a salesman and his prospect to leave with the promise of seats at the Grand Charity Ball and a heart-rending story about Jade and her family needing privacy to discuss a 'personal tragedy'. Then he'd bustled about like a mother hen taking orders for coffee. Samantha demanded chips and sausages.

'I always come to the Motor Show. Every year.' Wayne's face was the picture of injured innocence.

'I love your dress.' Lee-Anne had the same besotted look as the fans queuing up for her autograph. Jade almost preferred the bitchiness; at least it was real.

'I can't stay long, I'm here to work,' she said.

Then, seeing the disappointment in Sam's eyes, she added, 'How's Mum?'

'Fine, now you're gone. Dad hardly ever loses his temper so she doesn't get as many migraines. But Marlon's got diarrhoea after eating all the roast pork at the Gorilla Motors barbecue, and the twins have been expelled from kindy for fighting.' She stared up at Jade. 'I want to ask you something.'

Just then, a boy with serious acne, and a hair net on under a paper cap, came in weighed down by food. There were steak sandwiches, pies, sausages smeared with ketchup, bottles of coke and an enormous bowl of chips. Another plate barely contained a mountain of lamingtons, scattering coconut like dandruff. The spotty boy turned to go.

'Where's my Perrier?' Jade commanded.

'Sorry,' he faltered, suddenly recognising who she was. 'I'll run out and get some.'

'I wish I got service like that.' Wayne looked up, chewing a lump of meat.

'Are you really going to eat all of that?' After weeks of sushi and starvation, Jade's stomach lurched at the sight.

'Do you good to eat a few chips,' he mumbled, pouring out ketchup in a thick red stream.

'Jade, I want to ask ...' but Samantha was struck dumb by the sight of Daniel at the door.

'Here you are. I heard your family were here. Hello,' he strode forward, hand outstretched, 'I'm Daniel Hunter. And you,' he paused smiling 'must be Jade's brother?'

Wayne coughed up a piece of gristle. 'No, mate. Just a mate.'

'He's my *ex*-boyfriend, and she's my *ex*-girl-friend,' Jade cut in crisply. 'This is my sister Samantha.'

Samantha went pale. 'Would you like a lamington?' she faltered, holding up the plate. He cheerfully munched one, asking which of the new cars everyone liked. Conversation had never been Wayne's strength, but that question opened the floodgates. A sheaf of glossy brochures was produced from Lee-Anne's snakeskin handbag, and Wayne launched into the benefits of a decent European hydraulic system. Daniel winked at Jade and looked enthralled. Lee-Anne leaned over the table with her arms crossed so that her breasts almost fell out of her dress. Samantha's eyes were bulging like a shocked pekinese.

'. . . and that's what me Dad reckons, and he should know, been running Gorilla Motors all his life.' Wayne concluded, sitting back happily and stuffing a wad of chips into his mouth.

'And do you work there too?' Daniel inquired politely.

'Since I left school. Jade did too, detailing work. And she was the Gorilla Girl,' he added proudly.

Jade sat up straight. 'Isn't it time we left?'

'I can see you as a gorilla girl.' Daniel's eyes lit up with wicked amusement.

'And she was Miss Dairy Queen,' Lee-Anne

chipped in, glad to be able to contribute.

'Really!' he smiled broadly, 'I'd love to be able to see the photos.'

'I've got a life-size cardboard cut-out of her in my room,' Samantha joined in. 'I pinched it from the deli.' Then, seeing the interest in Daniel's face, she went on, 'She's wearing a white bathing costume and a stupid face and holding up a carton of cream. I hang my hard hat on it.'

Jade shrank in her seat; it was going from bad to worse to bury-me-now. But Daniel was in his element.

'So, Samantha, you like riding?'

'I love it,' she breathed, eyes glittering.

'Then you must persuade your sister to bring you down to my farm one weekend. I've got the perfect pony for you. In fact, there's no one to ride him these days, you can have him all to yourself if you like.'

Samantha looked close to fainting. 'What's he called?' she whispered.

'Follow Your Dream, but his stable name is Percy. He's thirteen-two and a Welsh-Arab.'

Her mouth formed a little round 'O', but she couldn't speak.

Wheels appeared and snapped his fingers. 'Come on, luvvies. Places to go, people to meet.' A cameraman followed him in. 'Oh, and before you go, a quick snap of the family?' he smiled.

'Who for?' Jade scowled. Wheels was up to something.

'*The Picture Post,*' said the photographer. A greasy little man with a head like a boiled egg was already setting up a mobile light reflector. 'I've paid for it,' he added, glowering at Wheels, who vanished out of the door.

Lee-Anne giggled and put her arms round Wayne and Daniel, and Samantha boldly plonked herself on Daniel's lap. All four grinned cheesily into the camera.

'Am I the only sane one here?' Jade fumed. 'This story could end up wedged between "I was abducted by Alien Transsexuals" and "Crazed Teenager in Suburban Sex Triangle."'

'Sounds like the story of your life,' grinned Daniel, giving Samantha a big hug.

'Come on,' Lee-Anne implored, 'join in. I've never been in the papers before.'

'The shot's no good without Jade Silver!' The boiled egg waited impatiently.

Of course she had to give in, and as they were leaving she could hear Samantha launching into a colourful description of living with Jade.

'My reputation is finished now,' she groaned.

'Nonsense.' Daniel held open the fire door into the street outside. 'Your sister is delightful; I wish I had one like that. Now Wheels said he would pick us up here. Ah, there he is.'

She squinted in the daylight. Wheels and his driver appeared smoothly at the kerbside. Flicking open the doors, he bared his teeth and told them, 'Tonight is the big one. Got some real high flyers turning up. The Premier will be here, and some very heavy money men. The Board have got a fantastic celebrity list set up. Afraid you guys only rated table twenty-seven, but believe me, thousands didn't even get an invite!'

The Grand Charity Ball! As if today hadn't been enough. As soon as they reached the Regent, Jade excused herself, dashed up to her room, locked the door and collapsed on the bed groaning. Her feet were swollen from the six-inch heels, her cheek muscles ached from smiling all day, she was hot with embarrassment over stupid Wayne and Lee-Anne. And Daniel still hadn't made a move. *He must think I'm some stupid kid from Borringup!* she concluded, rolling herself into a tiny ball. *He'll be offering me a pony next.*

An hour later, she struggled into the bathroom to start the whole dressing performance all over again. *Once I could shower, brush out my hair and dress in six minutes flat,* she thought nostalgically. There was a radio speaker on in her bathroom playing seventies revival music to commemorate the Frothing Alsatians World Tour, 'Rabies Rising'. *There's no tomorrow,* she sang along tunelessly, *just rage today.* Then the DJ announced he had Alevin in the studio for an interview. Jade pricked up her ears. 'When were you last in Australia?' The DJ's treacly voice murmured reverently. 'Dunno,' said Alevin. There was a long pause. 'I fink it might have been ten years ago, or twenny.'

He's stoned, thought Jade. *I wonder where Scarlett is?*

'And how does it feel to be back?' the sycophant continued, undeterred. 'Orright, I suppose. The chicks are orright.' There was a familiar giggle in the background. Then the DJ introduced 'the lovely Scarlett Stone, star of "Sunshine Coast" and Alevin's current companion.' He asked her what Alevin was really like.

'I never talk about my private life,' Scarlett replied. She was trying to sound mature. 'We're just good friends,' a pregnant pause, 'for the moment.' Alevin chuckled.

Jade glanced at her watch. *Not much time left, in a lot of ways*, she thought ruefully. Tonight was her last chance with Daniel. Tomorrow it would be back to work and with their hectic schedules, she might never get another chance. *No more Miss Dairy Queen*, she decided. *I should take a leaf out of Scarlett's book; she obviously knows what she's doing. Trust her to get a radio interview with the biggest rock name in the world. A change of tactics, that's what I need.*

She strode purposefully towards the wardrobe and pulled out the white, floor-length gown. *Thank you, Ivan,* she murmured. It was perfect. A satin Studebaker with built-in cups and slashed to the waist. A collection of faux jewels held the dress together at the chest and thigh. It was outrageous and perfect with her height and colouring. *It's not what you've got,* Scarlett had advised, *it's what you do with it.*

129

Jade slipped into the matching fluffy swan's-down bolero and examined herself critically. *Scarlett would be proud of me. He's got no chance tonight!* She swanned down to the lobby.

Daniel was waiting for her under a vast chandelier that quivered like diamond jelly. Beside him a space-age, scarlet Ferrari revolved on a black velvet dais. The interior shimmered in silver leather, almost as brilliantly as the gleaming engine exposed to public view. *Almost indecent*, Jade thought, *like a beautiful girl with her knickers down*. But Daniel wasn't looking at the engine; he was reading a brochure. She watched him for a moment: his cool, detached gaze, his hair like polished ebony falling across his forehead. She crept closer, hoping he wouldn't notice so she could enjoy the sight of him in a black tuxedo. Her pulse quickened.

Finally she spoke, 'Are you thinking of buying it?'

The expression in his eyes was a wonderful confidence boost. But he said, 'Hello, Miss Furry Queen,' and tucked the pamphlet into his pocket. Jade noticed a picture of a horse on the cover. *The only man in the world who doesn't care about cars*, she thought. *Or women*, she added miserably as he ushered her towards the ballroom, one hand impersonally gripping her elbow.

A wall of security guards blocked the entrance. Wheels materialised. 'Everyone's uptight. Rumour has it the Frothing Alsatians might show,' he said, and led the way, nodding like a conspirator at the chief guard.

'Make a good profit today?' Daniel asked as they followed him into the Ballroom. Jade didn't hear his response, her senses assaulted by the sight of thousands of tables festooned with golden helium balloons. Thick carpet deadened their steps, waiters shimmied past carrying flaming platters. In the distance a forty-piece orchestra played theme songs from old Hollywood movies. And everywhere feathers, jewels, starched linen, crystal goblets, laughter and perfume.

'Our table,' he announced with a flourish. Daniel pulled out her chair and sat down to her right. Wheels slipped in on her left. Craning her neck, Jade tried to read the name card beside Daniel. Something long and foreign-looking. 'Champagne?' Wheels didn't wait for a reply. Daniel started up a conversation with a matronly woman opposite who turned out to be a romance writer. Jade loved her books and was dying to join in the conversation, but Wheels monopolised her.

'The thing about fuel injection is the fantastic thrust you get!'

Jade yawned. He droned on and on and on. Apart from the mystery foreign woman, the table had filled up, so the waiters brought hors d'oeuvres. Jade stared at her plate. A miniature Rolls Royce, black and glistening, sat on a bed of ice with the Motor Show logo stamped out of a piece of toast. A baby tomato beside it, looking like a rose with the skin peeled back for petals. *Poor little tomato*, she thought, poking at the car as it crumbled into black caviar. Daniel behaved impeccably, filling and refilling her glass with an expressionless smile.

Right, now or never. She cleared her throat.

'Daniel?'

He put down his knife and fork and looked at her. She cast wildly around for inspiration. Out it came.

'Do you like me?' How lame, how pathetically schoolgirlish, how dismal, how degrading, how sad . . .

'Yes.' One hand plucked hers from her lap. They stayed motionless, wordless, facing each other. Like the eye of a hurricane, thought Jade. A kaleidoscope of light, colour and noise swirled around them. And the two of them peaceful at the centre. There was no need to say anything. The pressure and warmth of his hand was enough.

'Darling!' A face appeared. Jade blinked. Standing before her was the tallest, thinnest woman she had ever seen, her heart-shaped face framed with glossy raven curls. A miniature black satin slip dress exposed miles of smooth brown skin, as if she'd been dipped in milk chocolate. Daniel snatched his hand away.

'Juanita! What on earth . . . '

'Am I doing here? I've come to see you, *chéri*. Do excuse us, we're old friends.' She flaunted her perfect teeth at Jade and sat down. One slim brown hand automatically reached for the nape of his neck and caressed his hair. Jade felt sick. The tiny tomato stared up at her, unblinking. She stabbed it with her fork. *Stupid tomato, rejected, like me.* Swallowing hard, she stifled a sob. Wheels, ever the opportunist, asked her to dance.

'No, thank you, I . . . ' She stood up unsteadily and rushed away, searching desperately for the loo. Juanita Santiago! That was the name she'd read in the magazines. Belinda had said something about an old girlfriend. *So that's the reason he keeps us all at arm's length. He's been crazy about that, that, anorexic witch! And I've made a total fool of myself all day, every day, flirting and flaunting and thinking I could interest him.* Her cheeks flamed, a solid lump formed in her throat, and tears blurred her vision. Stumbling, she lurched towards an arch draped with red velvet.

'Sweetie! Your face is bright red. Where's The Man?'

Scarlett's loud, slurred voice startled Jade. Looking wildly around, she made out a table full of dishevelled musicians, and someone in a green Afro wig who looked a bit like Scarlett. Beside her lounged Alevin Starr, his feet on the table. He was watching her with interest. Scarlett raised a heavily chained arm. A studded dog-collar round her neck was attached by finer chains to a studded leather bustier. Her lipstick was black.

'Come here, darling, and help me cope with these mad pommies.' She was drunk.

Jade blew her nose. 'What are you wearing?' she hissed.

'My polish is red, don't worry. This,' she waved blood-red talons over her black leather mini-skirt and three-inch thick platforms, 'is just for tonight, to celebrate the boys in town. Boys!' She swayed to her feet and smashed a crystal glass against a magnum bottle of Bollinger to attract their attention. 'I want you to meet a mate of mine.' Then, abruptly, she fell back into her chair, smiling lopsidedly, before crashing her head onto her caviar car and falling asleep.

'Gone to bye-byes.' Alevin flicked out a starched napkin and tucked it over her shoulders. Jade looked into the famous bloodshot, slate-grey eyes. He was incredibly handsome and going to seed with sexy bags under his eyes and creases like duelling scars down his cheeks. His hair, back-combed and blond-streaked, looked like a wig. He stared too long, then let his eyes wander slowly down her body. She was horrified to discover it excited her.

'Who are you?'

'Jade.'

'Jade, Jade, let's get laid,' he chanted, then tipped up the chair beside him so that a plump blonde in layers of pink chiffon tumbled to the floor like a blancmange, then rolled away. 'Sit down!'

'Animal!' Jade snatched back her hand and turned to go. 'Scarlett,' she shook her shoulder, 'we're going. Wake up!'

'You're right,' he agreed, smiling languidly,

'bloody boring party. This place is a cemetery, let's go.'

Jade glanced despairingly towards table twenty-seven. She could make out Daniel and Juanita, heads together deep in conversation. Scarlett screamed. Someone had poured the rest of the Bollinger over her head and she was sitting upright, one half of her face speckled with caviar. Deep-green fronds like seaweed dripped down her cheeks.

'I'm coming too!' Her black lips pursed a kiss to Alevin, then she struggled out of the chair, found one of her platform shoes and limped purposefully towards the exit. Alevin put on his sunglasses, drained his glass, jerked his head at Jade, and followed.

I can't leave her alone; she's totalled and he's a maniac, she thought, rushing to catch up with them. She squinted in the half light to see Daniel and Juanita on the dance floor, moving in slow circles to 'I Will Always Love You'. Jade stifled a sob and stumbled out, past the security guards, through the foyer and out into the damp night air. There she found Scarlett weaving around uncertainly, gulping fresh air and claiming to feel better. The discarded wig lay dead on the pavement. Alevin's chauffeur held open the door of a stretch limousine. He was already inside.

'Come inside, babes, and let Daddy look after you.' He popped open more champagne.

The back of the car was as big as Jade's

bedroom in Borringup. Scarlett threw herself full-length along the back and twined her legs around his neck. 'Jade doesn't drink champagne, do you, babecakes? Give me that dead rat you're wearing,' she commanded.

Jade slipped off the swan's-down bolero, and watched aghast as Scarlett dipped one end into her champagne to wipe her face then guzzled back the rest of the glass.

'Don't be a spoilsport,' Alevin said, handing Jade an extra large one.

The familiar Melbourne streets rushed by, blurring into a long grey tunnel broken by street-lights, strobing the shadows. Jade's eyes blurred and her hand holding the champagne shook uncontrollably.

'How was the concert?' she asked to be polite and hide her fear.

'All right. Didja go?'

'No, we had . . .'

'She was being a good li'l girl and helping Marshall promote his stupid show.' Scarlett hic-cupped and held out her glass. 'She's a suck!'

'Is that right, Jade?' There was a soft insinu-ating note in his voice. His eyes glittered danger-ously. 'Is that what you like to do?'

Terrified, Jade downed her glass and shivered.

'You need something to warm you up. Try this.' He fished in his pocket and handed her a tiny jewelled box.

'What about me?' Scarlett struggled upright

and snatched it. 'Eckies! You're a legend, Al.'

'Have been for years,' he smirked. 'Steady on, Scar, share the sweets around.'

Jade looked at the tiny white pill left in the box. The others had swallowed theirs and were watching. *If I hesitate now they'll know what a complete dork I am*, she thought. *It must be Ecstasy. Juanita probably puts them in her coffee.* At the thought of Juanita, tears welled up in her eyes again. She swallowed the pill.

The car ground to a halt. Alevin leapt out, barking instructions to a pair of burly security men. Suddenly an engine roared and the air thrashed, sending gusts of diesel into the car. This completely disorientated Jade, who was struggling to retrieve her sodden bolero. Then Scarlett tumbled out of the car onto the tarmac. Jade followed as propellors revved, beating the air and whipping her dress up to her thighs. Her hair smashed around her face as if she was in a blender.

'This is bizarre,' she said, the wind snatching her words away. 'Where are we?' she tried again. She wondered how one little pill could affect her senses so powerfully.

Scarlett, bent double, was weaving unsteadily towards the open door of Alevin's Lear Jet, her feet bare and a champagne bottle tucked under her arm. Large men in dark glasses talked into mobiles in a huddle around him. He brushed them aside and grabbed her hand.

'Come on, babe,' he roared, picking her up as

if she were a toy, 'you are going to find out the meaning of the word "party"!'

'In an airport?' She was seriously confused.

'In Sydney, stupid!'

10

Alevin, in goggles and headphones, took the pilot's seat. Scarlett was wedged in next to him and Jade sat by the window. One of Scarlett's chains caught in the joystick and since she was dissolving in hysterics, neither of them noticed the plane rocking wildly from side to side as it lifted diagonally into the air, engines roaring.

How beautiful, thought Jade, dreamily. The airport lights swam in front of her eyes, zigzags of colour. Peering up, she could see stars, millions of them, universes of them. *Here am I, Jade Silver from Borringup, sailing up into the heavens with Alevin Starr. This is the stuff fantasies are made of.* Glancing over, she could see his profile, serious now as he flicked buttons and switches, making flip remarks into a mouthpiece strapped to his chin. His body, lean and tightly muscled, sat loose in the chair. He was obviously in full command of everything and everybody. *Like a king*, she thought, *with his courtiers and wives*. It made her feel proud to be one of them.

Soon they were lost in the black, velvety night. Scarlett's head lay heavy on his shoulder, smelling faintly of fish. She was snoring. Jade was in a different dimension. Images floated past of crowds shouting 'Kerry' and queuing up to gaze at her, and Sammy sitting on Daniel's lap, and the Evil Queen gloating and towering over her, all black hair, eyes and heart. And then the world standing still as he held her hand. A solitary tear rolled down her cheek.

'Penny for 'em.' Alevin's hand reached over and gripped her knee.

'I lost him,' she whispered.

'There's plenty more fish in the sea. Depends if you want tiddlers or sharks.' His wide familiar smile promised a world of fun. 'What do you want, Jade?'

Suddenly tiny bubbles of light exploded behind her eyeballs. A surge of euphoria erupted. She wanted to sing out loud. Instead she shouted, 'I want everything! Fame, love, money, stars in the sky, helicopter rides, more champagne, little white pills, and all the fish in the sea.' She giggled.

'Everyone does, darlin', until they get it.' But he spoke so softly she couldn't hear.

'I want caviar cars and Paradise Towers every day of my life and fabulous parts in major inter-national blockbusters and the whole world to scream my name and my face on the front cover of every magazine. I want to party till I drop.'

'Thass my girl,' mumbled a comatose Scarlett.

'You've got the right guy.' He yanked at the joystick, sending them freefalling crazily down in space. 'Coming in to Sydney now. The Kennel, two one four.'

Most of the rest of the evening was a blur. More security men met them at the airport, then they were driven with motorcycle outriders and sirens blaring all the way into Double Bay where Alevin claimed to know a 'groovy scene'. It turned out to be the private mansion of Sydney's leading show-biz entrepreneur. Scarlett jerked upright as they drew up at marble columns and outsize fountains.

'Where th'hell are we?'

'Party for me mates, gotta new album out. Coming, dolls?'

Jade gazed enraptured at the coloured spangled lights cascading round the fountain but Scarlett, like a true professional, snapped into action. Snatching Jade's purse, she found a comb and lipstick. Seconds later, her hair fluffed into shape and a new mouth painted over the smudged black one, she emerged, head high, to face a dispirited looking group of photographers slouching on the limestone wall, smoking roll-ups.

Gripping Alevin firmly by the arm, she marched towards the grand entrance. Lights flashed and bulbs exploded as the photographers scrambled

141

to capture the most exciting photographs of the evening.

'Look this way, sir.'

'I'll bet Mrs Starr is frothing this evening!'

'Has Scarlett joined the Alsatians?'

Jade drifted after them, unnoticed.

'I'll be in all the papers tomorrow,' Scarlett grinned gleefully. 'Aren't you glad you left Mr Goody Goody with that evil-looking clothes horse? Give up on him, he's nuts about her, always has been. Here, have another Ecky.' She shoved a pill into Jade's mouth and rushed off after Alevin.

Then they were inside. Alevin grabbed Jade's arm and pushed through the evening-suited guests, oblivious to the waiter who dropped a tray of canapes, the society matron who choked into her double gin, the famous model damaging her neck craning to see, the entrepreneur's wife who fainted in memory of a one-night stand in London in the seventies. Jade, who was still attached to him by the grappling hook hold he had on her wrist, floated dreamily in his wake.

'Jade, you're supposed to be in Melbourne!'

She glanced back to see an irate Marshall swallowed up by the crowd. Alevin halted in front of the live band and thrust a glass in her hand. On the dais she recognised one of Australia's oldest and most successful rock groups. The lead singer, about to launch into the opening number, spotted Alevin and leapt down.

'Al, fantastic! We're doing your number, take

the mike and wake up this herd of zombies.'

Alevin released Jade. 'Stay here, babe, where Daddy can see you.' Then he whooped, threw the mike in the air, signalled to the band, and exploded in a series of contortions and wild yelps that sent the room into a frenzy. The band exuded a suffocating stench of dope and sweat, hairy armpits spilling out of black sleeveless shirts. Jade swayed to the music, floating into the mass of undulating bodies. Felicity's face swam into view.

'What are you doing here?' Jade asked, confused.

'He's my secret lover,' she whispered at the top of her voice, pointing towards the wealthy entrepreneur. 'I call him Arthur.'

'He won't be a secret much longer!' Scarlett appeared suddenly and as Felicity disappeared, she asked, 'Her face is familiar, who was that?'

'Our make-up artist,' Jade answered, surprised.

'I never remember crew.' Scarlett's black leather and chains clanked off in pursuit of the singer, who was watching Alevin enthralled.

Finally the number ended and Alevin stood in front of her, piercing the confusion with his powerful gaze. For a while they danced, his snake-like movements and hypnotic stare mesmerising. She felt as helpless as a kangaroo caught in a spotlight. Through a fog of cigarette smoke, she could make out jewelled matrons and girls with white skin and scarlet lips, men with designer stubble and leather jackets. Everyone was pretending not to look at Alevin because it wouldn't be cool to be impressed by fame, but staring surreptitiously all the same. They stared at her as well, the vaguely familiar face of a girl who had the famous Alevin Starr, the greatest living rock legend in the world, eating out of her hand.

'Hungry, babe?' he asked pulling her aside.

'No.'

'Hang in there.' He pushed his way through the crowds towards the exit. The Australian rich and famous melted in front of true royalty. 'Because it's time for action.'

Terrified and excited, Jade followed him back out to the waiting car. Once inside, he rapped out orders to the driver and took her in his arms as they screeched off into the night. Through half-closed eyes, she saw the streets of Sydney melt into a blur of speed and intoxication. His mouth clamped over hers and she was powerless to resist. She didn't even try. Then she was in his arms again inside the Lear Jet, and there were stars outside. The next time she looked, they'd become the lights of Melbourne. After that, she remembered nothing until she woke up in an unfamiliar bed, in a penthouse suite.

A band of steel bound her head, throbbing at the temples. She opened her eyes tentatively, making out a darkened sky through the uncurtained windows. It was a ghostly early-dawn purple. Then she thought of Daniel. Somewhere he would be lying in Juanita's arms, probably tangled in her

144

endless limbs, she thought nastily, before a wave of pure desolation washed over her. There had been a magazine article about her in *Cleo* last week. 'The toast of New York', they'd called her. Belinda had tried to hide the article. *Oh, God*, she moaned, *how will I ever face him again*.

Various sounds in the room convinced her she wasn't alone. Gingerly, she raised her head. The bed was empty, but on the sofa opposite, she could see the almost-naked body of a plump blonde, curled up in Alevin's black satin jacket. No sign of Scarlett. The last time she'd seen her, she had a mike in her hand and was marching up and down the stage singing 'Like a Virgin'. Was that in Sydney or Melbourne? She swung her feet out of bed, and immediately knocked over a bottle which clanged against a glass. Someone moaned 'belt up'. The sound came from a pile of coats and blankets on the floor. A large glass bong on the bedside table was filled with sludgy stinking water. The ashtray beside it overflowed. Jade's stomach heaved and, struggling upright, she staggered towards the bathroom, tripped over another body and made it to the toilet in time.

When she finally stopped regurgitating and was lying exhausted on the bathroom floor, shame took over. What on earth happened last night? Through the fog, the only thing she could remember was getting out of the car outside the hotel. The onyx sink and gold taps convinced her she was still in the Regent, but whose room was it? Scrambling to her feet, she peered at herself in the mirror. Her hair, half down, was fuzzy and tangled, mascara ringed her eyes like a giant panda and her dress, chic and unusual last night, looked like something a drag queen might wear in a Kings Cross cabaret. And she thought she might vomit again if she could bear the pain in her throat, which felt as if it was swollen up like a puff adder.

The shower helped. Towelling off, she wrapped her hair in a turban and picked through the debris for something to wear. The best she could find was an acid-green chiffon man's shirt, and a pair of black leather men's jeans which fitted perfectly, apart from 'unzip here' embroidered along the flies. Barefoot, she tiptoed out of the room and made her way down to the foyer.

'Good morning, Miss Silver. You're up early!'

It was the Chinese concierge who knew Daniel. Thank God he recognised her. 'Morning. May I have my key, please?'

'Puke green is not the best colour for this time of the morning.' Alevin stood smirking lazily in front of her, his slept-in face and sleepy eyes as potent as ever. 'Particularly since we're goin' out for breakfast, that is if there's anyfink open in this graveyard.' He turned towards the concierge.

'Sorry, sir.' Recognising Alevin, his almond eyes swelled into perfect circles. 'Too early, everything closed.'

'Come on, sweetheart, we'll cab it to the beach

and watch the sunrise, and then I'll unzip here.' He made a grab for her trousers.

'No taxis, sir!' Anxiety was rising in the concierge's voice. 'So sorry!'

But Alevin was unstoppable. Striding towards the open-top Ferrari still revolving slowly on its platform, he helped Jade into the passenger seat, closed the bonnet and found the key in the glove compartment. Struggling to fit it into the ignition, he yelled, 'Switch off the bloody revolving motor before I vomit on your carpet!'

'Cannot, cannot, sir, this not our car. For display only.' The concierge was almost in tears, clutching at the bonnet as if to hold it back. Alevin fired the ignition and a roar of acceleration echoed round the foyer.

'Please, please, I lose my job,' pleaded the concierge, kneeling in front of the dais.

'Settle down, I'll buy it. Here.' Alevin pulled out a cheque book and wrote a cheque for a quarter of a million dollars. Then he thrust the gearstick into first, let out another roar which sent the concierge diving for cover, and drove off the dais, pausing to let the sliding doors open.

It was early dawn. The deserted streets of down-town Melbourne reverberated with the super-tuned roar of the Ferrari. Banks, hotels, office blocks flashed by faster than the speed of thought. Jade's thought, anyway. Somehow, she'd lost the plot again.

'What's going on?' She found her voice at

last, husky from squeezing through her flaming, infected throat.

'Just a li'l drive.' He shot through the red lights at the bottom of St Kilda Road. 'Beach this way?' he asked, and put a hand on her thigh.

Jade removed it. 'About last night, where did we go after we got back to the hotel?' She tried to sound casual.

'Had a bit of a party in our suite, the boys came up, and some friends.' He put his hand back on her thigh, and overtook a startled pantechnicon driver on the inside lane of the south-bound freeway.

Jade held her hand firmly over his. 'Did we do anything, I mean you and I?'

Alevin looked bored. 'Can't remember, but I fink you passed out. Better luck tonight, eh?' Wrenching at the gearstick, he shot past a tractor, an inter-city coach and a Porsche in one swift roar of noise.

Jade was so relieved, she started to laugh, then clutched at her throat in agony. A police car drew up alongside them as they paused at a railroad crossing.

'Can't stop, officer, my girlfriend's pregnant, and we're late for her abortion.' The crossbar swivelled up, and he roared off. The expression on the policeman's face! Jade burst out laughing. The sun was rising, hot-pink streaks setting the gum trees on fire. A flock of parakeets lifted noisily from a paddock. They were into open countryside now.

The road grew straight and fast as he opened up the throttle.

'Nice motor. You can have this when I've finished playing with it. We're off tomorrrow, going to Japan. Ain't got any decent roads there.' He had to yell now, the words whipping past in the wind. Jade felt the strain of it on her neck as they built up speed.

'Did you say I can have it?' she screeched, paralysed with fear and excitement. A sign saying '100' in big black figures flashed past – the speed-limit. The countryside was rushing dizzily. Struggling to focus, she made out the speedo. The needle flickered up to two hundred.

'Shouldn't we slow down?' she screamed hoarsely, but Alevin pumped out another roar of acceleration and her words were lost. Up ahead, on a side road, two patrol bikes faced them. As the black car shot past, they turned, sirens blazing in pursuit. Jade could see them in her rear-view mirror, like matched bookends. 'They want us to stop,' she roared.

'Shan't! First decent drive I've had 'in months.' Alevin stuck his right foot down hard on the floor. The motorbikes shrank out of sight. 'I won!' He cheered up, switching on the radio.

Jade felt herself relaxing. The car was built for speed, the rich leather bucket seat held her, thick grey carpet stretched out underfoot. She pressed a button and her seat sank back, giving her a staggering view of the sunrise. The sun, burning ochre-yellow low in the sky, hovered motionlessly. A Beach Boys song rose jubilantly over the noise of the engine. A guilty, irresponsible pleasure lightened her mood. She glanced over at him. Like a naughty child, he hunched over the wheel, intent on squeezing the Ferrari to its maximum. *He's quite sweet*, she thought, watching him fumbling with a cigarette lighter and a crumpled joint, steering the wheel with his knee. *Well, harmless, anyway. And one of the most powerful men in the world.* She hugged her arms together. *And I've got him! Sucked in, Daniel Hunter!*

'What's so funny?' he asked, blowing a plume of smoke into her face.

'Not that,' she answered as a shadow suddenly appeared overhead. A police chopper swung down across the road, hovering above their heads. 'This is the police, slow down immediately, you are approaching a road block,' boomed the loudspeaker.

'Happening!' whooped Alevin. 'Hold tight!'

Jade screamed. Looming ahead were several police cars and motorbikes. A large flashing sign ordered them to stop. Uniformed men grouped purposefully around an iron swing bar.

'Stop!' she screamed. Jade caught sight of their startled faces before she closed her eyes and held tight. The Ferrari lurched, spinning violently one minute then straightening amidst the sickening crunch of buckling metal, before roaring off again. She opened her eyes. The first thing she saw was

Alevin, wiping away the tears of laughter. It was the only time she'd seen him really animated. Twisting in her seat, she saw the barrier lying tangled by the side of the road, and one of the policemen on the ground.

'He might be hurt.'

'Only a slight knock. It's his own fault. Would you stand in front of a speeding Ferrari?'

Jade agreed with the statement, but there was something wrong with the ethics. She felt uneasy and looked towards him for reassurance. He was slowing down and the familiar bored expression was back.

'I'm starving,' he complained, re-lighting his joint.

'We're near an old hotel, one of the early settlers' places.' Jade had some misgivings about Alevin in the shabby genteel surroundings of the White Rose Hotel, but her stomach was rumbling louder than the Ferrari in first gear. 'Turn left here.'

The tarmac gave way to gravel as the road twisted deeper and deeper into hillocks of blue gum and acacia before veering off steeply into a valley of roses. Jade was enchanted. The air filled with the perfume of lavender and rose and bee song.

'Bloody pollen,' he sneezed. 'Why don't they just concrete over this lot?' He pulled up with a jerk in front of a grand Federation-style house, flanked by two vast Moreton Bay figs. A marma-lade tabby snoozed in the shade, nestling in the thick roots of the fig tree. Jade leapt out and knelt down to cuddle it.

'Don't touch that cat!' he shouted. 'I'm allergic to cats.' Then, striding up the steps, he clattered hard on the door. A window opened on the second floor.

'We're closed, come back at nine.' A grumpy woman in curlers stuck out her head.

'I'll give you a thousand dollars to make us brekky.'

'You're mad.' The head retreated.

'Okay, sterling, a thousand pounds!' he yelled.

The window opened again, and a man's head appeared. 'I'll be right down!' And soon a pretty table was set up in the rose garden, where the morning sun shone on the silver and porcelain. He made them delicious pancakes with maple syrup, fresh peaches and figs, and crispy bacon in warm bagels. Jade tried her best to be interesting and witty, but Alevin munched silently, pausing occasionally to drag on the lighted cigarette he kept near his plate. Studying him in the bright morning light, she could see a grey re-growth in the blond-streaked and back-combed hair. His skin looked dull and unhealthy, and a petulant curve pulled down the corners of his famous lips.

A single helicopter that had been swooping around for some time, turned and headed off back to Melbourne.

'They've gone, all clear. We can go now,' she added.

'Nah. My gig's not on till later. We'll stay.' He took out a pill bottle and swallowed a handful, washing them down with black coffee. Then, planting a hand on her knee, he said, 'Spect we could bribe him for a room.'

The headache that had pressed behind her eyeballs all morning suddenly swam into full view. Irritation flared. *Why am I putting up with this like a beaten housewife? I've been a wimp with this man since I met him.* Disgusted with herself, she stood up.

'I want to go back to the hotel,' she said and without looking back, she marched off towards the car. She thought of Daniel and his gentle concern and had to suppress a pang of longing. It was all so wrong, being here with this old man who treated her like a prostitute. She half expected him to offer her money to stay.

As if on cue he shouted, 'I said you can have my car tomorrow when I leave.'

Fuming, she turned to face him. 'You think you can throw money around and get anything you want!'

'S'right. I do, because it works.' He slowly got to his feet and slapped a wad of notes down on the table. 'I can pull any bird I want, I can do anything I want wiv money.'

'How do you know if people really like you, then?'

'I don't care, as long as they give me what I want.'

Jade climbed into the car. Alevin fired the ignition. She asked, 'So if you have zillions of pounds and always get what you want, you must be very happy. Right?' She looked at him sideways, under her lashes.

Pulling out a piece of silver foil from his pocket and holding it to his nostril, he sniffed loudly. 'Lost me there, doll, what did you say?'

Jade repeated her statement slowly, to which Alevin, a broad grin slowly creeping over his craggy face, replied 'Blissed out.'

Saddened, Jade sank back in her seat, arms tightly folded against her chest.

They saw no more choppers, but as they made their way into the outer suburbs, she thought she caught sight of police cars at various intersections, watching them flash past. He'd turned the radio up to full quadrophonic sound and the station was playing a heavy metal special. Her headache was now a serious, suitable-for-hospitalisation migraine.

It was at one of the main side roads that turned into Regency Street that the accident happened. A wispy-haired mongrel was loping diagonally across the road, ears at half-mast, with a cheerful silly grin and lolling tongue. Jade caught the details like a snapshot the moment before a soft thud hit the fender. Then the slightest of bumps as they bounced over its puny body and roared off down the street at twice the normal speed.

'Stop,' she croaked, 'it's hurt!'

'Not hurt, doll, splattered.' He changed gear

and swept into the drive of the Regent Hotel. 'In Canada, I squashed a whole moose with a snow-plough at two hundred miles an hour.' He faced her proudly, yanking at the handbrake. 'Miles that is, not kilometres.'

Jade stared at the seedy washed-out blue eyes swimming behind folds of wrinkled skin. They were expressionless and mirthless, despite his smile. A cold shiver ran up her spine. *He's not even really there*, she thought in disgust.

Suddenly it all became clear. All that fame and adulation and money! She remembered how it felt signing all those autographs, the way people looked at her, as if she was super-human. And she had begun to see real life, through the tinted windows of taxis and Cadillacs, as nothing but distant images.

She'd walked away from her family last time, angry with them for not paying her enough atten-tion, ignoring the pain in her mother's eyes. Her grandfather was dying, and she had forgotten all about him. And she remembered the bitterness in the street kid's eyes as he clawed at her face, enraged at the unfairness of life.

Where did it all end? With the crumpled body of a stray mongrel, crushed for fun? She stared into Alevin's empty face, seeing no sign of life. She shuddered in horror.

There was a sudden explosion of light as a camera flashed, then another and another and another. A crowd of reporters swarmed around the car.

155

'Miss Silver, how was the ride?' That came from the tarted-up, middle-aged harpy who ran the show business section of 'New Faces'.

'Al, are you taking up racing driving?' Jade recognised the *TV Times* reporter.

'Did you know the police are waiting to interview you?'

'Any comment?'

'How did you feel when you knocked down the policeman?'

Pushing through the reporters, Jade shielded her eyes from the brightness of the flash bulbs. Over Alevin's shoulder, waiting in the foyer, she could see Wheels ringing his hands nervously, a group of very plain-clothed detectives and Daniel with a face like thunder.

'Daniel, quick,' she rasped, ignoring Wheels, who had immediately launched into a whinge about Marshall. 'There's a dog, just round the corner. We ran over it.'

'Will it live?' he asked, shouldering away the reporters crowding around Jade.

She nodded, her voice reduced to a whisper.

'What are we waiting for, then?' He grabbed her hand, and they set off at full speed down the drive.

11

'Thank you so much for helping me.' Jade whispered to Daniel. They sat in first class on the afternoon Sydney flight later that day.

'I wasn't helping you, I was helping Brando,' he whispered back, checking to see if there were any stewards around.

Jade zipped back an inch of her bag and peered into the dark. A soft steady breathing reassured her. Cupping her hand gently round the head of the little animal inside, she closed her eyes and tried to calm herself. The last few hours had been unimaginably horrible. The press had been bad enough; God knows what they would make of her day out with Alevin, and that poor policeman. What would Marshall think? Worst of all, what would Scarlett say, or do?

Then there was Brando himself. By the time they'd reached him, he'd crawled to the edge of the road, his leg bent back and a trickle of blood coming out of his mouth. The vet said he'd been lucky to survive, set his leg in plaster and gave Jade some special animal tranquillisers. Then they'd searched for his owners. But without a licence number, there'd been little chance of success. So she bought a special carrying case and hid Brando. Going back to the Regent, she bumped into Alevin in the lobby as she waited with Daniel for a cab. He didn't seem to recognise her in jeans and no make-up. She tried to tell him about the stray dog, but he was surrounded by fans and the security men made her feel like a groupie. I don't suppose he cared anyway, she thought bitterly, about Brando, or me.

Glancing sideways, she studied Daniel's profile, but she could read only contempt. Her heart sank.

By the time they touched down at Sydney, Brando was waking up and her sore throat was almost unbearable. They only just made it through the security checks in time. Falling into a taxi, she unzipped the bag and stroked his shivering, scrawny body. 'Not long now, darling, we'll soon have you in a warm bath and into bed.'

'Sounds as though that's what you need,' said Daniel twisting round from the front seat to watch. 'When did that cold start?'

'I don't know,' Jade sneezed, 'today I think. My throat's sore.'

'Driver,' Daniel ordered, 'pull over there.' He

jumped out and disappeared into a deli. Jade found she was shivering more than Brando; at the same time her face was burning. Struggling to find her father's gold compact, she flipped open the top and peered at her face anxiously. As she suspected. Fire engine red! Daniel flung open the back door and handed in a bag. Four tins of My Pet Chicken Dinner for Loved Puppies, a bottle of Flea Shampoo, a packet of spaghetti, tomato sauce, mozzarella cheese, a tin of soup, a bottle of aspirin, throat lozenges and a litre of cough mixture.

'I haven't got a cough.'

'You will soon, judging by the state you're in. Give me Brando, he'll have to be hidden!'

They drew up outside Paradise Towers and Ben came smiling out to open the door. 'Miss Silver, what happened? You look like death.'

'Thank you, Ben. I've been to Melbourne.'

'That explains it,' he laughed, rushing to summon the lift. 'My brother once went to Melbourne and he . . .'

Daniel pressed the 'close' button firmly. 'I'm coming in with you.' His face was set in stone.

'There's no need,' Jade coughed, 'I can manage.'

'Like you've been managing all weekend?' They stepped out of the lift and Jade only just made it to her door. Stumbling in, the first thing she noticed was a putrid smell coming from the kitchen.

'Straight to bed,' he pushed her towards her door. 'I'll deal with the dead body.'

She crawled into her room, peeled off her clothes and discovered her bra and pants soaked with sweat. Once in bed, her teeth going like castanets, she was overcome by waves of volcanic heat one minute, drenched in cold sweat the next. She could hear him in the kitchen opening a can of dog food and speaking softly to Brando. The next moment he was beside her, taking her temperature with a face like thunder.

'What did that old bastard do to you?' he muttered, heaping a pile of blankets onto the bed and rustling around for pills and water.

'Nothing, I hope.' She could barely speak through her chattering teeth.

'I'm going to run a bath for Brando in the sink; he needs to be de-flea'd. Those pills will knock you out, but I'll be here until you wake up. Okay?'

Gratefully, Jade sank under waves of sleep, rolling over her like the ocean, blotting out the pain. She dreamed she was on the roller-coaster from Hell, swirling masses of horrific sights and sounds through furnaces and walls of fire. Waking suddenly, the first thing she saw was a pair of beady honey-coloured eyes. A tiny tail thumped against the blankets. Her sheets were damp and sticky hair clung to her forehead. At the window, she could see Daniel in her armchair, reading scripts. Silhouetted against the light, his face in the shadow was impossible to read. Jade struggled upright and swung her legs onto the floor.

'Where do you think you're going?'

'I'm going to the toilet, by myself,' she mouthed, hoarsely.

'Not without a dressing-gown,' Searching the room he came up with a large towel and his own sweater.

When she flopped back into bed, he came over to tuck in the sheets and stroke a thick strand of damp hair off her forehead. Jade wished he'd stop staring at her. Flushed, sweaty, mute, no eyebrows or lashes, smelly hair. After the Toast of New York *I must look like a bad dream*, she thought. *He's probably congratulating himself he didn't get involved with me.* A fit of coughing drowned out the depression that threatened to take over. Brando's tongue rasped her arm.

'He's so cute,' she said, reaching out of the blankets to stroke him.

'Stay under the bedclothes!' he ordered.

Jade looked up crossly. Alevin, my step-Dad, now Daniel, she thought. Bloody men think they can control your life. Sitting up on one elbow, she put all her energy into croaking, 'Stop bullying me.'

A brief smile flickered across his face. 'Looks like you may be ready to eat.' Then he disappeared into the kitchen, returning with a tray of chicken soup, water and some brown bread.

'What happened last night?' he began, spooning soup into her mouth and holding a napkin under her chin to catch the drips.

'Scarlett and Alevin and I left, after Juanita arrived.'

He looked uncomfortable for a moment. 'I didn't see Scarlett.'

'She was wearing a green wig and black leather bondage gear. Not so fast, my throat is sore.'

'Sorry, and maybe you shouldn't talk anyway.'

'The heat is helping. We went to Sydney in his Lear Jet.' She stopped to swallow another mouthful. Brando was interested, his head flicking from side to side with the movements of the spoon.

Daniel looked stern. 'Then what?'

'Some party, to launch the Stone Masons' new album, at Joe Connelly's mansion. That's enough. Can I have a drink?'

'Water. You've had enough champagne for the year, and possibly a lot of other things besides.'

Jade drew back, trying to look as dignified as possible with a napkin bib, greasy hair and no make-up. 'All I had was a little white Ecky or two.'

'From Scarlett?' he frowned.

She nodded. 'And Alevin.'

'That's what I was trying to warn you about. It would suit her purposes to have you into drugs. Do you know what our ratings were for last week? The highest for over a year. And all because our audiences have a girl they can relate to, an innocent, average girl. How long do you think your dewy-eyed fresh look will last once you're hooked into the Sydney club and drug scene?'

'Audiences love Scarlett!' She was stung as much by the implication she was an ordinary suburban nobody, as the attack on her friend.

'She knows how to handle it. She's the leader of the pack. Haven't you wondered why so many of our new faces disappear so suddenly? When Scarlett's threatened, she either terrorises the competition into leaving or, if they're too strong, she befriends them and finds their self-destruct button. Everyone has one. We had a delightful girl once who was picking up fan mail and ratings like crazy, until Scarlett discovered she had a police record.'

Jade closed her eyes. Her head was throbbing like a heavy-metal band. So Scarlett never really liked her, and it was obvious Alevin only wanted her for sex. And Daniel, despite acting like a friend, had kept Juanita a secret all this time. Who could she trust?

Opening them again, she saw him disappear into the kitchen with the tray. His jacket lay on the armchair. There was a wallet bulging with papers in the inside pocket. Stealthily, she slipped out of bed and made her way over to the chair. The wallet was stuffed with receipts and old photos. The first one she pulled out showed Juanita and Daniel in formal evening wear. They were both laughing into the camera. *I'd do anything*, she thought, *to make him look as happy as that.*

Replacing the wallet, she glanced over at her reflection with horror. Her piggy eyes disappeared under folds of puffy red skin. Damp strands of hair, dark with sweat, lay on her shoulders, and bundled into his sweater she looked about eighty kilos.

'What are you doing?' He walked back into the room, his face an angry mask. 'I turn my back for one minute and you're preening in front of the mirror like the rest of the empty-headed girls in television.' He stalked in and gripped her by the wrist. 'Into bed, now!'

Jade jumped quickly under the covers.

'You know, when you first arrived on set I thought at last we'd got a real actress. Someone natural, talented and strong enough to resist the pressures of fame. Now you're peering at yourself in mirrors all the time, wearing Penthouse clothes and looking out for the next famous person to be photographed with. You're as shallow as Scarlett!' Turning on his heel, he stormed out of the room.

Jade stared after him, breathing hard. Brando started to whimper. She raised her voice as hard as she could. 'Look what you've done. You've upset Brando. He'll grow up insecure now!' There was no reply. Tears of frustration stung her eyes. I won't cry, she resolved, reaching for more tablets. I won't cry.

After that, she must have fallen asleep again, because when she woke up it was dark. Brando was snoring on her pillow. A large envelope was propped up on her dressing-table. Gingerly, she crossed the room and pulled out the letter.

Dear Jade, it read. *I waited until your temperature went down. Your dinner is in the oven. Eat it. Brando's been fed and I've removed a stinking*

164

mushy lump of mould from your fridge. See you tomorrow, Daniel.

The flat suddenly seemed lonely. Shuffling down the hallway, she noticed how quiet it was, how empty. Well, I don't need him, I don't need anyone, she thought defiantly. And he was right about one thing, I'm an actor. I've got this far, the Plan will work. I'll survive without any of them! But somehow, she wasn't so sure the plan was such a good idea any more.

There was an enticing smell wafting in from the kitchen. Spaghetti Bolognese, dripping with melted cheese. She didn't realise how hungry she was. Dragging the duvet into the sitting-room, she made a bed for herself on the sofa, switched on the TV and settled down to watch the news.

'Megastar Alevin Starr of the Frothing Alsatians,' read the announcer, 'completed the final leg of his Australian tour with a farewell appearance in Melbourne.' The clip of Alevin thrashing around on stage made Jade want to vomit.

Then the film switched to a. scarlet Ferrari drawing up at the Regent. And there was Alevin, flashing his index finger at the cameramen, pushing his way haughtily through the crowds. The voice-over intoned that an accident had occurred on the south-bound freeway when Alevin and his companion Jade Silver, Miss Dairy Queen of Borringup and a newcomer on 'Sunshine Coast', had driven through a police block and caused what at first appeared to be a hit-and-run accident. A shot of Jade showed her nervously pushing her way towards the hotel entrance, shielding her eyes like a criminal.

Finally a senior policeman was interviewed. He explained that Mr Starr, without Miss Silver, had made a special visit to the injured man's bedside to wish him well, and that the injuries were slight. No charges would be pressed, in light of the fact that Mr Starr had offered to pay all costs involved and donated a 'generous' sum to the police fund for injured victims of hit-and-run accidents.

'I am quite sure this was not a hit-and-run,' the policeman explained solemnly. 'Mr Starr had no knowledge of Sergeant Smith's accident due to heavy weather conditions. We also believe Miss Silver assured him the road had been clear.' Then the newscaster showed further clips of Alevin setting off for Japan, surrounded by thousands of cheering fans, like a national hero.

Wearily she reached for the zapper to change channels, then went rigid. There was Juanita Santiago striding down the catwalk, smiling seductively into the camera, as sinewy as a panther stalking its prey. And Jade knew who that was. The newsman raved about a major Australian fashion show attracting 'some of the loveliest girls in the world'. Suddenly, she could hold back the pain no longer. *The world's Beautiful People*, she thought bitterly. *Alevin Starr would beat a murder rap with bribery, Scarlett Stone is the friend from hell and that, that person has stolen the only man I've ever loved! And they've all got the morals of a cockroach!*

Struggling to her feet, she crossed to where her mail was waiting. Daniel must have picked it up on his way out to see Juanita. *Leaves me here dying so that he can hold hands with her in some cosy hideaway.* She blew her nose loudly and pressed her fingers hard into the corner of her eyes to stop the tears. Crying only made her eyes puffy and piggy. *Better read scripts for tomorrow.*

The fattest envelope held late revisions from the scriptwriters. Underneath was an official envelope and a David Jones bill. She opened that first.

'What!' Gasping in horror, she stared at the Final Amount Due – $2,673.99. Her heart sank. The next was from the management of Paradise Towers to say that her month at the expense of Channel 6 was about to expire and, assuming she would be staying on, enclosing a bill for the next month, $2,500. Jade reeled in a fresh spasm of coughing. Where on earth would she be able to get her hands on so much money? She didn't even know how much her salary was. Reaching for the phone, she dialled her agent in Melbourne.

'Jade, whasser matter?' He sounded as though she'd woken him out of a deep sleep.

'I need to know how much money I make,' she croaked.

'At this time of night? What's wrong with your voice?'

'Nothing. How much are they paying me?'

'Well,' he sounded evasive, 'you didn't seem

too interested in money at the time, so . . . '

'How much?' Jade was frantic.

'Award rates,' he mumbled apologetically.

Jade slammed the phone down. It was worse than she thought, and she only had herself to blame. I've screwed up, she admitted to herself. If only I'd listened to him. The phone tinkled, and she snatched it up.

'Treasure, I've just seen you on the late night news. Not the best PR, is it?' Belinda was sympathetic.

'Do you think Marshall will have seen it?'

'He'll find out about it. There could be twubble.'

'Oh, Belinda,' Jade broke down, 'I'm in so much trouble, and not just that.' She poured out the traumas of the weekend, her financial problems, and Daniel's accusation against Scarlett. 'Do you think she really was befriending me to destroy me?'

'Scarlett never does anything unless it's in her own interests,' Belinda agreed. 'I've been worried about you. Particularly now.'

'What do you mean!'

'She'll have seen the news. How do you think she'll react when she hears you went off with Alevin today?'

'Was she the serpent in Paradise you warned me about?'

'Not really; I was talking about fame. What it does to you. What it's done to people like Alevin. When you live in all that luxury, you start to think you're above evewything, that you can do whatever you want. Alevin and Scarlett are simply amoral. They're like children, taking what they want, and because they're famous, they get away with it. That's why I moved in with my Gran. Helping her use the loo and cleaning her false teeth keeps me weal. Otherwise I might end up believing all the media hype.'

Jade felt chastened. 'What do you think Scarlett will do? I mean, nothing happened last night with Alevin!'

'How can you be sure if you were stoned?' Belinda let that sink in, then added, 'You know, Daniel really has a thing against drugs.'

Jade sank to her knees and curled up in a foetal position on the carpet. 'Oh God, oh no, what shall I do?' she moaned.

'Did you manage to explain it all to Daniel? It seems to me you never had a chance against Alevin.'

'I was too sick, and he was too angry with me. Anyway, he rushed home to Juanita.'

'Oh dear.'

Jade dropped the receiver back onto its cradle and began to howl, great rasping sobs that filled the air. Then she rolled over onto her stomach and beat the carpet with her fists. How desperately unfair everything was. Now her life was in ruins. All spoilt, all her lovely fantasies about acting, about making it on her own, about winning Daniel's love. Rocking from side to side, she wept as if her heart would break. She no longer cared what she might look like tomorrow. *There may not be any tomorrows; I'll probably be sacked for bringing the show into disrepute.* Another wave of agony shuddered her body. *I'll have to go home to Borringup and beg Giorgio for my job back. Oh no, help me, help me,* she moaned, gasping for air. Hardly able to breathe any longer, she flopped back exhausted, every bone in her body aching.

A tiny thought started to grow at the back of her mind. 'Mum. I want my Mum,' she said out loud, and blindly groping for the phone, she dialled reverse charges and asked for Borringup.

'Mum? Thanks for taking the call. I'm short of money.' A lump the size of a grapefruit seemed to be lodged in her throat.

'Darling, what's the matter?' There was so much love in her voice, Jade broke down again. For some moments she wept silently into the phone.

'That's okay, baby, just breathe deeply. Wait until you're ready to speak.'

Then it started to come out, slowly at first, then in a rush. Margaret Silver listened silently, asking questions occasionally when she became confused. Not once did she sound shocked or worried or critical.

'Are you alone now?'

'Yes, but my temperature's gone.' Jade blew hard into another tissue. The pile on the floor looked like a snowman. 'Isn't this call costing thousands?'

'It doesn't matter.'

They carried on talking until Jade found herself yawning.

'I want you to go to bed now,' her mother soothed, 'then call in tomorrow and tell them you won't be in for the rest of the week.'

'You don't understand,' Jade wailed, 'you have to be dead before you can get time off. Even then, they'd prop up your dead body and dub your lines.' They both giggled.

Later, in bed, Jade was surprised to discover how much better she felt. *My mother may not know much*, she thought as she drifted into a paracetamol-induced sleep. *But at least she accepts me as I am. And I think she loves me.*

Not many people seemed to love Jade Silver at Channel 6 the next day. 'Miss Groupie Queen' was lipsticked on the Green Room mirror. Red lipstick. No prizes for guessing who wrote that. *And it must have been Daniel who told her*, Jade thought wearily. *So much for chicken soup and watch out for Scarlett. He's as bad as the rest of them.* Belinda had no scenes that day, so there were no allies to bolster her confidence when the call came through. 'Jade to Marshall's office, immediately!'

Marshall was in his office drinking coffee and dragging on one of his old Indonesian cigarettes.

'I thought you were on a health kick?' Jade tried sounding cheerful.

'I'm on an arse kick,' he glared up at her.

'Your arse! What the hell do you mean by associating our show, our happy clean-cut families with hit-and-run accidents, stolen cars and that revolting old rocker. He could be your father! And all on national news.'

Jade suppressed the thought that they must both be the same age.

'What the hell happened anyway? You look bloody awful. How did you end up in Sydney when you were supposed to be in Melbourne?'

She was about to tell the story yet again, when the door burst open. It was Maggie, waving her bangles around and grinning from ear to ear. 'Febulous news, darlings. Admin. say the switchboards are jammed with callers. The world and his wife wants to know if Kerry has abandoned Jason for Alevin Starr! You're a romantic heroine, Jade, you're on the map!'

'But nothing remotely romantic happened, with either of them. With Daniel it's only ever been acting. The other was a fiasco!' Jade never ceased to be surprised by audiences thinking her character was real.

'It's the perception that counts.' Maggie lit a cigarette and reached for a bottle of champagne. 'Kerry has been seen with the greatest living rock legend. Fame rubs off, darling. You're big, now. Really big. And the ratings are set to soar. Bubbly?' She held up the bottle. Jade shook her head.

'I've got to learn lines. I had flu over the weekend; my throat's still sore,' she mumbled, backing out. Not to mention another migraine threatening to attack.

'Before you go, this came for you.' Marshall handed her an envelope with the logo of the Regent Hotel. Oh, God, another bill. They're catching up with me for the mini-bar she thought, stuffing it into her handbag and rushing off to the toilets to swallow more paracetamol. Her face looked like a traffic accident, so she hid it behind sunglasses and headed off to see if Felicity could salvage anything in time for her first scene.

'Trying to disguise yourself?' A sharp voice rang down the corridor. Scarlett stood blocking the way, her blood-red lips curled in an ugly sneer, the local tabloid paper gripped in one claw.

12

'Scarlett's Night of Shame' screamed the headline. Jade took the tabloid from Scarlett's fist. The photograph showed a close-up of Scarlett with unfocused bleary eyes, lipstick-smeared cheeks and hair tangled like a mad woman's. The dog-collar and chains were clearly visible. She glanced briefly at the article. There was a reference to the 'beautiful newcomer Jade Silver and her companion, Alevin Starr'. But most of it discussed the lure of drink and drugs and the dangers of young, highly paid actors becoming involved in substance abuse. There was also mention of the practice of bondage and speculation about Scarlett's sexual preferences.

'So?' Jade struggled to suppress fear and a desire to giggle.

'Who did you sleep with to get this, this . . . ' her hand shook as she rattled the paper in Jade's face, 'scurrilous garbage published?'

174

'Well, it's fairly accurate. The bondage may be over the top, but then again ...'

A low hiss escaped from Scarlett's lips. 'You miserable specimen of low life, you revolting slag, sliming away behind my back ...'

'I did nothing! You were the one who charged forward to get your photo taken with Alevin! I didn't force you to drink too much or take all those pills.' Jade suddenly snapped. 'Although the same can't be said for you! You're the low-life, setting me up to take stuff I couldn't handle. And as for that disgusting Frothing Animal, the last thing I wanted was to be stuck with him for the night. You know perfectly well I've always loved Daniel, and you set me up to fail at that as well! And you talked me into buying a swag of horrible clothes that make me look as ridiculous as you, and bankrupted me.' The blood was pounding in her brain, but she couldn't stop. 'All you've ever done is try to destroy me from the moment I arrived, only I was too stupid to see it.'

Scarlett went as white as a gothic, her mouth a tight slit. Just then, the production assistant appeared.

'You're supposed to be on set, Jade. Scarlett, Marshall is looking for you.' She winked at Jade and took Scarlett by the elbow. Daniel, about to emerge from the men's changing rooms where he had been standing silently for the last ten minutes, retreated again.

'Oh, Felicity, it was horrible,' Jade lay her

head on the make-up table and moaned.

'Come on, darl, we've got seconds to sort your face out.' She hurriedly patched up Jade's skin and eyes, listening to the story of her fight with Scarlett and her day with Alevin.

'You did the right thing. No one's ever had the nerve to stand up to Scarlett before. Her ratings have been so good, Marshall always caves in to her. Whatever Scarlett demanded she got. Public approval has been her power base. But after this article, she could well lose it. And thank God for that. She's a great little actor, when she's not on her star trip.'

Jade's face looked almost normal again. If only her head wasn't crashing around like the Frothing Alsatians. 'You think we'll be able to work together again?'

'No choice, she'll have to get over it, and she's a tough little cookie at the end of the day. Best thing that ever happened to her,' she grinned. 'No pain, no gain! And before you go, you never saw me on Saturday?'

'I saw nothing,' Jade smiled gratefully. 'Wish me luck.'

She didn't know how she survived the next few scenes. Most of the other actors had heard of the weekend, teasing her mercilessly, and not always kindly. The technicians were wary, they obviously thought she was going the same way as Scarlett. At one point she thought she might faint under the heat of the spotlights.

'You'll soon cool off this afternoon,' the

director said. 'We're shooting that pool sequence today instead of next week. Yet another re-write.'

'I can't,' Jade was aghast. 'I've got flu. I can hardly think straight as it is.'

'Sorry, orders.' He switched on a fake smile of apology and bustled off, chatting into his mobile. Jade scrabbled about in her handbag for pills. Three paracetamol left. She swallowed them all. The fever was threatening to break out from under a cement layer of foundation as she set off in a taxi for the pool location shot. There had been no sign of Daniel all day, and he wouldn't be in the last scene either. The sense of desolation was awful. I have never been so utterly alone, she thought.

A small crowd gathered round the 'Sunshine Coast' vans outside the private pool they'd hired. The moment she stepped out of the taxi she was mobbed by excited schoolgirls. Their bubbly pleasure only made her feel worse. They seemed to think her life was incredibly exciting, filled with glamorous men and wild parties. If only they knew!

Felicity was waiting for her in the make-up van, ready to do a full body.

'Hold still,' she complained, 'I can't work when you're shaking so much.'

Unable to wear a wrap, Jade shivered by the pool for over twenty minutes.

The light and sound men were having a hard time with bad atmospherics. 'It's degraded, too weak, too weak,' the sound man yelled as they completed the checks.

'Don't I know it,' she muttered, teeth chattering.

Rain clouds were grouping and deepening to the colour of tarmac. The scene required her to stand waist deep in the pool and carry on a quarrel with Scarlett, who would then splash Kerry in fury. Jade had no lines, apart from a cry of anguish. It couldn't have been worse. *If I'm not dead with flu by the end of this, I'll have lost my voice yelling, or been poisoned by the purple hate smoke that Scarlett sends out invisibly. Suicide would be a fun option*, she thought, stepping into the freezing water.

She watched Scarlett emerge from the van, rugged up and haughty. She began by complaining about the glare from the water.

'Not used to daylight, are you?' the third assistant director said boldly.

Jade waited for the explosion. Nothing. Scarlett calmly took off her robe and waited for the clapperboard. The first take aborted when water splashed on the outdoor mike.

'It sounded like gunshot,' the technical director's voice boomed through the intercom.

Jade wondered if shooting was a possibility. She watched Scarlett nervously for signs of a weapon. But the scene wrapped on the fifth take with no problems at all, apart from a raging fever galloping through Jade's nervous system and a migraine like a volcanic eruption.

'Put this on, you look like a cadaver,' Scarlett threw her robe at Jade.

178

Jade thought she must be hallucinating. A kindly gesture, after everything they'd said to each other? Maybe Felicity was right. 'Thank you,' she managed through teeth rattling like a kookaburra.

Scarlett grinned unexpectedly. 'Just make sure it's dry-cleaned when you return it!'

'Thanks,' Jade managed to smile back. It was as if a great weight had lifted off her shoulders. They walked back together to the caravan, Scarlett moaned about the third assistant director having 'no respect'. Everything forgotten.

Later, when Jade had showered, shampooed and been quickly blow-dried by Felicity, and smothered in a huge pink mohair sweater Belinda had left in the make-up van, Jade finally crawled back into the studios to pick up her call sheets and bag. It was dark in the Green Room, most people had gone home, and the phone was ringing urgently. Jade picked it up.

'Jade? It's me, Samantha.'

'You okay?' Jade was surprised out of her daze.

'I want to ask you something, but you never have time to talk to me.'

Jade felt crushed. She could picture the little anxious face; she knew how much Sammy idolised her. 'I'm sorry, sweetheart. What can I do for you?'

'I want to get into TV, like you, Jade. Can you help me?'

There was a silence. She listened to the child breathing heavily, intent on her answer. 'Finish school first. Get the best grades you can, then we'll talk about it. Okay?'

'But that's what Mum said,' Samantha whined, 'I want to do what you did!'

'It's too dangerous. Tell you what, work hard and I'll let you come and stay with me next hols.'

'And ride Daniel's pony?' The voice squeaked up several octaves.

'Sure. Goodnight,' and she dropped the receiver back in its cradle. *If I can bear to carry on seeing him, being treated like his baby sister,* she thought miserably, lurching off down the corridor to the exit.

There was a light on in Marshall's office and the sound of raised voices.

'You mean you let them shoot the pool scenes today, when the temperature's down ten degrees and that poor girl's in the early stages of serious pneumonia!' It was Daniel in a towering rage.

'How was I to know she was sick?' Marshall defended.

'She was in here earlier. Maggie told me she looked terrible. Don't you ever look at your people?'

'We had to shoot, couldn't get the pool next week.' He was beginning to weaken.

'You won't have anything to shoot if she dies of neglect.'

'All right, all right, you win. I'll call her tonight and tell her to take tomorrow off.'

'At least a week, Marshall.' Daniel slapped the desk firmly. 'A week!'

'I can't give her a week, not with you off in Adelaide for three days. Isn't your flight tonight?'

Jade crawled past the door, hoping no one would see her. I was wrong, she thought, he sees me as a daughter, not a sister. She didn't know which was worse. Out in the carpark she searched for a taxi. But it was almost seven, and they'd gone. Swaying on her feet, her mind went blank. It was the final straw, she had no more reserves left to fight with. Nowhere left to turn.

'Jade?'

She looked back. Coming out of the studios, his large frame silhouetted against the streetlight, was Daniel.

He called out to her, 'Let me give you a lift.'

'I'll take a taxi, thanks,' she mumbled. 'You've got a flight to catch.'

But Daniel paid no attention; he walked right over. 'I'm taking you home,' he said, and gripped her around the shoulder, leading her towards the dusty Jaguar. His arm felt strong against her back. She no longer had the energy to argue. Heroine woofed softly in the dark, in greeting. The air felt like silk. 'How's everything?' he asked.

'You can stop playing big brother,' she whispered wearily. 'I'm okay now; it's all sorted out with Scarlett.'

'Who said anything about big brother?' They came to the car, but he hadn't taken his arm away.

She leaned her back against the car door.

Looking up at him, her face close to his, she felt extraordinarily at home. As if she could fall asleep just at this moment with his arm warm on her back and never wake up again. 'Oh, Daniel,' she sighed. She dropped her head onto his shoulder and rested her burning forehead against his sweater, breathing in the scent of cold night air and wool and sweat and lemons. Breathing in Daniel.

Moments passed.

A sharp nose nudged her back, followed by a whimper of impatience. Then Jade felt Heroine's tongue wet on her hand.

'Stop it, Heroine, you can't kiss her before me,' he murmured, tilting her chin up.

Terrified, Jade said, 'I never wanted to be with Alevin, you know, or take those pills, I didn't even know what they were ...'

His hand slipped down to her collarbone, pressing the skin beneath his touch as if massaging it back to life.

'It went well, today, the scene, I mean, with Scarlett.' She tried to ignore his fingertips trailing softly up her neck and circling her cheek and mouth. 'She even gave me her robe, 'cos I was shivering ...'

'You're still shivering,' he whispered, lifting the weight of hair from her neck and bending forward to press his lips against her ear.

'Daniel,' her voice a distant whisper, her skin electrified where he touched with his lips or his fingertips. She went on talking, desperate to keep control, a tumble of incoherent words.

'You were right about some of the things you said. I was starting to believe my own publicity, getting sucked in by all the hangers ...'

His mouth closed over hers, thankfully stopping the words. Jade felt herself drowning in a tidal wave of longing. She thought of Juanita. *No, no, no*. Bringing her hands up to his shoulders she pushed with all her failing strength, but it was like trying to stop nature. Her hands slipped over his shoulders, feeling the heat and strength of his back. And finally she gave way, holding him hard against her, kissing him back with every ounce of her being. And in the language of touching, she found what it was she really wanted to say.

'Now I'm taking you back to bed,' he released her very slowly. 'To sleep for a week.'

'I can't last for a week without you.' Jade fell into the passenger seat, exhausted and exhilarated beyond reason.

'Take your mobile to bed, and I'll call you from Adelaide.' He fired the ignition, and set off with a roar into the traffic.

'And when you come back?' She was gazing transfixed at the way his hair curled around the nape of his neck and up to his ear. Streetlights flickered past, lighting his profile. She swooned with love for him.

'I've got visiting rights for Brando.'

She giggled. Then she asked, 'But I thought you and Juanita . . . '

'Juanita? She's mad, bad and dangerous. I'm sorry about the way she butted in on Saturday. I'm partly to blame. I was still angry with her, had something to get off my chest.'

'What?'

'Well, a couple of years ago we were together. I was besotted with her, or who I thought she was. But she was only using me to get attention from the media.' He put out his hand and took hers. 'That's why I tried to keep my distance from you.' He grinned at her sheepishly. 'I thought you were too much like her, you know, too ambitious. You've no idea how hard it was to keep away.'

Jade felt herself blushing. 'I thought you weren't interested in me. Scarlett told me you still wanted Juanita.'

He sighed. 'Typical! Scarlett knew all about Juanita and the way she left me.'

'What do you mean?'

'She got a better offer, cleared her things out of my flat while I was out, and cleaned me up into the bargain. Almost three thousand dollars in cash I had ready to pay some bills. It wasn't the money,' he smiled at her. 'It was being used so callously. And I thought you were turning into another Juanita.'

'Give me your wallet and we'll see!' They both laughed. Then she added seriously, 'although I'd probably have to take five thousand dollars.'

He glanced across at her anxiously. 'Look, if you have any problems, I'd love to be able to help.'

'I'll be okay, I'll work it out.'

'That's what I really admire about you. You're a straight fighter.'

'More like a street fighter,' said Jade, and she told him about the poor crazy street kid.

Drawing up outside Paradise Towers, he took her in his arms, looking serious. 'Fame isn't to be taken lightly. You can't play with it one minute, then put it down the next. It sticks to you while you're in this game. And you have to respect the force it carries. Sometimes you attract dangerous situations. Promise me you'll be careful?'

Jade nodded.

'Now go on, get into bed before I miss my flight. I'll call you from the airport to say goodnight.

'Three days is forever.'

'Just make sure you eat properly and sleep all day. I want you happy and healthy.'

Jade didn't trust herself to speak. She kissed him hurriedly on the cheek and dashed in.

Brando rushed to greet her the moment she stepped into the apartment. Sweeping him up into her arms, she made for the kitchen. It didn't look right. To begin with it smelt clean, the sink was bare, and all the surfaces gleamed. A machine was humming in the laundry and there were sweeping vacuum tracks on the deep pile carpet into the sitting room where a bowl of white freesias danced on the sparkling glass table. The kitchen sparkled as well, all the debris of last night cleared away.

Wandering through to her bedroom, she found the satin bedspread shimmering evenly on the bed instead of puddled on the floor as it had been for weeks. A heater wafted currents of warm air into the room. Even the en suite gleamed, dirty towels replaced by fresh ones, lavender perfuming the air.

Then her mother walked in, wearing purple rubber gloves.

'I've put my things in the spare room. I'm staying until you're better.'

Jade gaped. 'But what about the twins? He'll never be able to cope without you.'

'He'll have to manage. Right now you need me.'

Jade stared at her mother, clutching Brando to her chest. Tears sprang into her eyes.

'Now into bed,' Margaret Silver suddenly sounded gruff. 'And give me that dog. He'll need a walk, I'll see if I can find a shop open. I'm going to have to buy some things, there's nothing but dog food in the kitchen.

'Oh, Mum,' Jade kept her voice steady. 'Thank you so much.' They looked at each other. 'I've missed you.' The minute she said it she knew it was true, even though she'd never thought about it before.

Margaret Silver peeled off her gloves. 'Jade, it hasn't been easy at home, since the other kids came along. And I know you never really liked your step-Dad, and there hasn't been much money to buy the things you wanted. But you never gave up on your dream and ... and I'm proud of you.' Then she blinked hard and bustled about to hide her embarrassment.

Jade slumped against the door, watching her switch off the washer and collect her things. She noticed her back, straight and dignified. She really is proud of me, she thought, tears rolling soundlessly down her cheeks. And it felt so good to have her here, to be a child again with someone to lean on. Gratefully, she limped back to her bedroom. Searching her bag for one last paracetamol, she came across the Regent Hotel bill. Might as well know the worst, she sighed, ripping it open.

Dear Miss Silver, Your Ferrari is still in the valet parking lot where it has been since Mr Starr left on Sunday afternoon. Our sponsors were somewhat surprised by the manner of the purchase, but since the cheque for $250,000 has cleared, and is considerably more than the original asking price, they are waiving their display rights and consider the matter closed. I am sending you the documents for your car and your receipt. Could you please arrange to have the car collected as soon as possible, or let us know where you would like it delivered.

Well, not Paradise Towers, anyway, thought Jade sinking back on to the bed and closing her eyes.

A letter from Isla

Dear Reader,

Thank you for buying my book! I hope you enjoyed reading it as much as I enjoyed writing it!

My heroine, Jade Silver, <u>isn't</u> me, but her experiences, in some ways, have been very similar to mine. Daniel Hunter is <u>not</u> Dieter Brummer or, in fact, anyone I know, but I wish I did. And of course there's no such person as 'Scarlett the Harlot', although she was great fun to write.

I started writing about the time I began acting, when I was thirteen. It's my own form of escapism. I never dreamed I'd be fortunate enough to one day have something published.

I love reading, particularly romance writers: Jackie Collins, Jilly Cooper, Danielle Steel — the tackier the better because I like the fantasy!

Working on TV isn't anywhere near as glamorous as the picture I've painted in this book, but you wouldn't want to read about how boring it really is — how early our 'calls' are and how repetitive filming a scene can be!

Anyway, my next book, which I'm finishing now, is about a friend of mine, a ballet-dancer who falls in love with a Hungarian gypsy whilst on tour with her ballet company. It's working title is 'Bewitched'.

I hope you loved reading 'Seduced by Fame'. Please write to me if you did, or if you have any questions.

I have started writing a newsletter about parties I go to and people I meet — it's a great excuse to gossip. If you'd like to receive it, write to:

Isla's Newsletter
PO Box 388
COTTESLOE WA 6011

All my love,

Isla

Some other Puffins

NOT DRESSED LIKE THAT YOU DON'T
Yvonne Coppard

'I asked David in for coffee, and he said yes. Great. I took him into the dining room, so we could talk without Mum and Dad gawping at us. Fine. We chatted, and I could see I was really making an impression.'
– Jennifer, January 6th

'Jenny brought her young man in for coffee. She was trying to look very assured and grown-up. She actually asked if we wanted some coffee, as if she were in the habit of doing these small favours for her poor ageing relatives.'
– Jennifer's mother, January 9th

'A wickedly funny book . . . This book is a must – easy to get into, impossible to stop reading' – *Independent on Sunday*

'Like all the best ideas it is utterly straightforward . . . astute and unpretentious' – Stephanie Nettell, *Books for Keeps*

SWEET DREAMS
Kate Daniel

When your real life is scarier than your worst nightmare . . .

Jan is terrified to go to sleep. Every night in her dreams she relives the blaze that killed her parents. As her dreams grow more vivid, Jan begins to suspect that the fire wasn't an accident: someone murdered her parents, and she thinks she knows who.

Then Jan starts walking in her sleep, finding herself mysteriously drawn to a series of midnight fires around town. At first the fires are small, but soon one of Jan's classmates – a girl who accused Jan of starting the fires – is horribly disfigured in the flames that destroy her home.

Is Jan's nightmare coming true? Is she an arsonist – and a killer too?

A PACK OF LIES
Geraldine McCaughrean

Story-teller, salesman and total mystery – who and what is MCC Berkshire?

Ailsa doesn't usually pick up men in public libraries – but then M.C.C. Berkshire is rather out of the ordinary and has a certain irresistible charm. Once inside Ailsa and her mother's antiques shop, he also reveals an amazing talent for holding customers spellbound with his extravagant stories – and selling antiques into the bargain!

'Sparkling with wit and originality' – *Guardian*

CHARTBREAK
Gillian Cross

'Right. Get this. While you're in the band, you're called Finch. Because I say so. And don't sing a note until you've got the sound of the band in your blood.'

When Janis Finch storms out after a family row, all she means to do is spend an hour or so drinking coffee in a motorway café. But then Rollo, Dave, Job and Christie walk into her life. They are Kelp, a rock band travelling to a gig, and Christie is their charismatic and demanding lead singer. An evening in their company is just the beginning of an exciting new life for Janis in the dynamic and hardworking world of the rock music scene.